VERY LIKE A WHALE

Very Like a Whale

A NOVEL

FERDINAND MOUNT

ff

faber and faber

This edition first published in 2010
by Faber and Faber Ltd
Bloomsbury House, 74–77 Great Russell Street
London WC1B 3DA

Printed by CPI Antony Rowe, Eastbourne

A CIP record for this book is available from the British Library

ISBN 978–0–571–25910–6

For Gideon Tode

HAMLET :   Do you see yonder cloud that's almost in shape of a camel?
POLONIUS : By the mass, and 'tis like a camel, indeed.
HAMLET :   Methinks it is like a weasel.
POLONIUS : It is backed like a weasel.
HAMLET :   Or like a whale?
POLONIUS : Very like a whale.

HAMLET, ACT III, SCENE II.

Chapter 1

The motorist, speeding westward from the complications of his London life, does not see much of Winkhill. A mile or so of monumental rhododendrons on either side of the main road, occasionally interrupted by lodge gates and a glimpse of winding sandy drives, and it is gone. Driving slowly, one may spot a forest of little signposts staked out by the lodge gates as in a botanical garden. Many of the names on the signposts indeed have a botanical connection – Hydrangea House, Laburnum Hill, Wisteria Cottage, Larchmount. Others are more geographical or literary – Montecristo, Hathaway Cottage, Sans Souci, Pontrilas.

The motorist, who misses so much cannot know what he has missed in by-passing Winkhill; what a variety of architectural styles ranging from mock Tudor to seaside Spanish; what a wealth of landscaped gardens, dotted with lily-ponds and exotic imported plants tended by exotic imported gardeners; and cementing it all together, the world-famous Winkhill golf course with its cultured fairways, its fine-sanded bunkers, its velvety greens. Here man has tamed nature; from his patio-lounge he looks out over his two acres of rolling garden and mixes himself the driest of martinis; he has learnt the secret of happiness – to cultivate his garden, or better still, to have it cultivated for him. Winkhill is, in short, a sort of Disneyland for adults. Those little signposts beckon to a host of civilized pleasures and expensive living.

> ' *Là, tout n'est qu'ordre et beauté,*
> *Luxe, calme et volupté.*'

Yet the darker side of human nature keeps breaking in. Civilization can only be maintained at a price, and the price at Winkhill is high. Spiritually and emotionally, it is tiger country. At Winkhill, stockbroker cuckolds stockbroker, American airline representatives drink deep and financier's wives and children wait trembling for the Fraud Squad's courteous knock at the door. Bodies, sometimes headless, sometimes not, are found in bunkers and divorce is commoner than marriage. To call Winkhill a sick society would be rash; after all what society can accurately be described as healthy? But Winkhill is certainly a society with a perpetual hangover. The successes in early life which enable its residents to become residents usually entail hard work and early hours; the excesses which Winkhill life demands militate against these. The arteries harden, the moral fibres slacken; prolonged mental and physical collapse and often premature death may follow. Winkhill does not encourage longevity. There is a market for desirable properties left vacant by owner's decease. And the market is always rising.

The third hole at Winkhill presents a wide classical prospect. Flanked by beeches, it sweeps downhill and to the left. Beyond a curving stream, the fairway rises to the bunker-girt green, suggestive of an incompetently excavated earthworks. Beyond are some substantial rhododendrons and beyond again, the bare skyline of Winkhill Heath.

George Whale, a heavy-built romantic young man, who was standing on the teeing ground, could distinguish only two features on that skyline – a pylon, the property of the Central Electricity Generating Board, and a single Scotch pine. On a clear day, one could see another pylon behind and to the right of the first, another in the long trail of aesthetic devastation bringing power to the Sussex coast. But today was not a clear day. The Scotch pine was shivering in the thin wind and would shortly be covered by mist. If, as seemed probable, the Pekinese, which was just visible urinating on the green, belonged to the Stettins, it would either catch pneumonia or have to abandon its claims to delicate health.

George Whale removed a lump of mud from his golf-ball, placed it on its tee and took up his stance. His cold hands interlocked round the club, like mechanically packed sausages. The disciplinary maxims of golf passed through his mind. Head down, straight left arm, pronated wrists. They must, however, have occurred to him in the wrong order as his drive veered well off the line and vanished among the trees on the right of the fairway.

As he set off in pursuit, George reviewed the shot and its failure. The difficulty was to know what caused what. Had his knees been too far in or his bottom too far out? As in some Zen interrogation, the answers bore no relation to the problem. His thoughts turned to the single pine on the horizon. The pine had figured in George's thoughts ever since he had left the Freudian shadows of infancy. It was the background to all the canvases of his imagination. As a US cavalry-man, he had passed that tree in the Colorado sunset, his blue shirt and breeches stained with sweat, his harness jingling. The pine had risen improbably out of the North African desert, as the Bedouin raiders attacked his dune-flanked emplacement. And, most important, in an educational comic, he had read at the age of ten the story of Roland at Roncesvalles. There had been a picture of the square-jawed Roland dying beneath a pyrenean pine with the silver-bearded Charlemagne on his knees weeping at his side. Study of Old French at Oxford had amplified this picture but not changed it. Nor had his earlier discovery of the squatters' camp behind the brow of the hill, a few hundred yards beyond the pine. Nor had the housing estate which now replaced the squatters' camp. Nor the railway below the housing estate which carried the able-bodied adult Winkhill males to London five days a week.

The pine remained obstinately lone, a symbol, both epic and elegiac, of independence.

' Count Roland lay under a pine tree. He turned his face towards Spain and thought of many things, of the many countries he, Lord Roland, had conquered, of sweet France, of the men of his line and of Charlemagne his lord who had brought him up.'

There was a strand of barbed wire concealed in the long grass at the edge of the wood. George's left foot caught it and he stumbled into a gorse bush. Two previously concealed figures rose like startled rabbits from behind the bush. One was his neighbour and contemporary, Ray Stettin, dark and lithe in a bright green tweed suit. George did not know the girl, who was obviously very cold. Her numb fingers had difficulty in doing up the buttons of her shirt. She would of course have been warmer if they had not been using her overcoat as a ground sheet.

' Hullo, George.'

' Hullo Ray, you haven't seen a small white golf ball anywhere?'

' No.'

' Must be somewhere.'

' Yes. This is Annabel Meyer. George Whale.'

' How do you do. Sorry to disturb you.'

Annabel was a thin girl, her cheeks, pink with cold and embarrassment. Her thinness was remarkable – more like a garden rake's than a greyhound's. She emphasized the vertical aspect of her face by a stockade of long straight black hair. Her fine dark eyes were rimmed with mascara. She had the undeniable charm of a half-starved panda.

' Hullo,' said Annabel.

' Hullo.'

Silence fell. George swung his niblick carelessly.

' Well, we must be getting on,' said Ray. ' We've lost Snooks. If we don't find him before dark, the little bastard will probably rupture himself.'

He spread out his hands to express the futility of looking for one Pekinese in a thousand acres of rhododendron.

' Good-bye George. We must meet soon. Why not come to a party we're all going to on Friday. It might be quite fun. We could eat first.'

' That sounds very nice,' said George, smiling at Annabel, who nodded.

' So long, then. I'll get in touch about Friday.'

' So long, Ray. Good-bye, Annabel.'

Annabel nodded. The pair walked off down the hill into the thickening valley mist. George went into the wood and stayed there for about five minutes poking at the carpet of leaves. He did not find the ball, a comparatively new

Dunlop 65. Coming out of the wood, he tripped over the barbed wire again.

George then turned for home, which lay a few hundred yards further on through the trees, by the tenth tee. The Whales had bought Larchmount when they got married. It was within commuting distance of London and it was what Cynthia Whale regarded as typical English country. As her childhood had been spent in Malaya as the daughter of a very successful rubber planter who loved the Old Country, this belief, though false, was important to her. Something of the Malayan landscape had perhaps crept into this childhood picture of England; hence her love for rhododendrons. Hervey Whale, then a rising young MP, had been easily persuaded into buying Larchmount, especially as Cynthia was paying.

Hervey was indifferent to his surroundings rather because his mind, left to itself, was idle than because it was occupied with some intense internal vision.

As Winkhill houses went, Larchmount was dull. There were no green tiles, no Spanish ironwork, no lattice windows. It was a plain house. Little could be said for or against it. Perhaps there was a little too much weatherboarding.

George parked his clubs in the lobby and ran the tap to wash his hands. He looked carefully into the mirror over the washbasin. Always interested in his own appearance, he had hoped as a child that his face might have undergone some startling improvement since the last check-up. This hope had faded. His face had settled into its pale, downward-drooping mould – the nose too long and narrow, the cheeks and lips too full, the jaw too shapeless. There was altogether too much face. His present narcissism was based on the belief that a shaft of light from some unexpected angle or some quirk of mood in the beholder might put a new complexion on the unchanging reality. He could then imagine that a pretty girl meeting him for the first time might happen to get this favourable viewpoint. The lobby mirror was known to be unflattering. After an unsuccessful inspection, George dried his hands and wandered into the hall, carrying *The History of Merchant Banking*, which he had providently left in the lobby before going out. The book had been given to him by one of the partners in George's bank who felt George needed encouragement.

The architect of Larchmont had solved his problems by abandoning them in the hall. All the darkness which had been rigorously excluded from the other rooms (for Larchmount had been built in the 1920's in the first flush of rediscovery of the fact that light comes in through windows) had collected there. All the sharp angles, niches and protuberances – resulting from the fine proportions of the other rooms – made the hall an inimitable shape. Hervey and Cynthia Whale had reasoned that this darkness and asymmetry could cover a multitude of wedding presents. As a result the hall had absorbed a grandfather clock, two brass coffee tables, an enormous Chinese vase containing umbrellas and walking-sticks, a large portrait of Great-Grandfather Whale in a large frame and other intolerable but unsaleable objects. It was of course the only room in the house with any charm. George had spent most of his childhood playing in it, preferring it with innate obscurantism to his bright, neat nursery. He had always disliked the nursery because of its wallpaper which featured pink and blue rabbits running in pointless pursuit of each other. The wallpaper had a shiny, washable surface.

The rest of the house was decorated in its adult equivalent.

It being too dark to read in the hall, George went into his father's study. Hervey usually spent Sunday afternoon preparing for any speech he might have to make in the coming week. It was a long-standing arrangement that George should disturb him at about this time. Hervey could read out the finer passages in his fine sonorous voice and George could dissect the more self-indulgent clichés. Hervey rather liked being told he was writing nonsense. His nonchalant agreement made him feel like the cynical *realpolitiker* that he knew he ought to be.

Hervey Whale was indeed writing his speech. His fine grave face watched his fine strong hand pushing the Biro across the paper. The pen moved regularly, even rhythmically. There seemed to be little connection between the brain inside his fine head and the words appearing on the page. He looked more like an elderly film star watching the ticker-tape machine in his club than one in the process of intellectual creation. Hervey was not in fact in the process of intellectual creation. He had given up creative thought when he first got into Parliament. A few last spasms of originality had been repressed when he joined the Government.

' George, what do you think of this? " Our party believes that each and every one of us should have the opportunity to develop his or her faculties to the utmost. If we are to build a classless, united Britain, this must be a first priority. But this is not just simple justice, it is a question of whether this nation survives, rich, prosperous and humane, or whether we perish and so deprive the world of our moral influence and example." Too Churchillian, do you think?'

' Not at all. Very rousing, in fact. I didn't know you believed in a classless society now.'

' Indeed we do. It's said to be the only slogan that will

attract the younger executives to our ranks. What extra-ordinary people they must be, these young executives. If only one knew what they meant by classless. It doesn't appear to entail stringing us up, or even taking our money away from us. That, I suppose, would be class warfare and very old-fashioned.'

' Isn't it,' said George cautiously, ' something to do with equality of opportunity?'

' So I believe, so I believe. But that unfortunately is a concept just as obscure to me. Still, one must soldier on, patching up the ship of state as one goes along.' Hervey's assumption of heroic perseverence was barely self-mocking. ' If you wouldn't mind leaving me now, George. I have to fit in seven minutes towards the end of my speech on the need for more technologists in Britain. That always goes down well.'

The Biro resumed its shuttling course, across the neat, octavo sheets. And Hervey's mind returned to the prison of received ideas from which it had cautiously peered forth.

Hervey Whale was Minister for Economic Co-operation. This job had been invented as a sop to the progressives in the Party. Economic Co-operation was clearly a good thing; there was not enough of it in an ideologically divided world; Britain must show the reality of her belief in the principle by appointing a Minister for Economic Co-operation with a small but high-powered team. Hervey was the obvious choice, superb in his Augustan appearance and his melli-fluity, familiar with the political and intellectual problems of the day without being bothered by them or wishing to solve them. Like a good defensive boxer who rides punches superbly without throwing any, Hervey could take change, even quite enjoyed it, but he never initiated it.

He was therefore installed as Minister in a large office overlooking St James's Park. On the wall hung a contemporary copy of a Canaletto lent by the Ministry of Works and a blown-up photograph of a strip-mill near Calcutta, presented by the Indian High Commissioner. This, as Hervey sometimes remarked to overseas visitors, symbolized the relation between civilization and the industrialization that was a precondition of civilization. It was his job, so to speak, to turn strip-mills into Canalettos.

Yet what in effect was his job? If people wished to co-operate economically, on the whole they did so of their own accord. When a Coventry firm signed a contract to build a hydro-electric plant in the swamps of Somaliland, Hervey expressed his delight. When the British Government started a minimum price scheme for tropical foodstuffs as a somewhat illusory encouragement for primary producers, Hervey said he was overjoyed. On the other hand, when the Estonians repudiated an agreement to buy tractors because the credit terms were too steep, Hervey said it was disheartening. When the British Government responded by cancelling a big order for Estonian soft wheat, Hervey noted the setback in Anglo-Estonian relations. It showed, he said, what a long way we had yet to travel. In fact, whenever the cause of economic co-operation took an encouraging step forward or a disheartening step backward, Hervey was there, applauding or deploring but not, unfortunately, participating. He exemplified the modern theory of government that by saying something often enough, it becomes true. Good modern-minded people read Hervey's speeches at breakfast and felt that a new spirit must be abroad in the world of trade. And if hard-headed men of business were turning towards Love and away from the base worship of Self, might it not be true of us all? Were we not all being reborn in a new Community identification? Hervey was thus both a perpetual sacrifice for our past sins of non-co-operation and a harbinger of the new age of Complete and Perfect Co-operation.

Hervey was fully aware of the questionable nature of his work. It rather suited him. He knew what was going on before most people. He was in the know. But he did not have to do anything about it. After all this was all that many apparently power-crazy politicians wanted. They liked the polished seat at the polished conference table, the ostentatiously secret ways into palaces and ministries (to avoid fuss), the ostentatiously unsecret limousines, chauffeurs and policemen (to create fuss), the caricatures which flatter by enlarging the personality. All this lifted Hervey above the common, commuting run of his Winkhill neighbours, it conferred on him a momentary, harmless immortality.

Power mania in this sense he did have, but organization mania which the man of destiny needs to reach the top and stay there, he did not have. In his previous job as Minister of Fuel and Power, decisions had frequently faced him. Sometimes he had chosen rightly, more often wrongly. One decision had resulted in a total and prolonged power-cut throughout mid-Wales at the height of summer. Civil Servants in his old Ministry spoke with respect, almost affection, of a man big enough to take such an obviously disastrous decision. But Hervey was quite a friend of the Prime Minister; he cheered the old man up and he asked for no favours as there was nothing he particularly wanted. So he was not sacked but transferred to the burgeoning Ministry of Economic Co-operation or the 'Mekon' as space-fictionados called it.

Here all was perfect peace. Hervey might go through a whole Whitehall day without having to take a decision bigger than whether to return to Winkhill before or after the rush hour. He found this no easier intellectually to decide than he would have found it to decide whether or not to declare war on Russia, had the occasion arisen; but it was a less exhausting choice.

' Five years ago, we only had 8,000 technologists in Britain,' wrote Hervey's pen merrily. Surely not, thought Hervey. 80,000 perhaps? Or 800,000? 8,000,000 sounded too many, but in a world where a ratcatcher was really a rodent officer, plumbers must be sanitation technologists, sweeps were chimney technologists and so on. The Italian who had spent the morning next door mending the television set was clearly a technologist even if he did sing Verdi with a confident flatness that shook the house. It all added up; there might be 800,000.

Hervey got up, walked across to his filing cabinet to look for his ' useful facts ' file. The cabinet was locked. He searched his pockets for the key. It was not there. He had left it in his tweed jacket. The tweed jacket was upstairs.

He stood for a moment, marvelling at the lack of forward planning which characterized his life. The time-and-motion man who had come sniffing round the Ministry and whom he and his colleagues had treated with fear and contempt, would not have left the key upstairs. He might even have questioned the value of locking a cabinet which contained nothing with any claims to secrecy. And in the first place, he would not have forgotten how many technologists Britain possessed. But Hervey was not the time-and-motion man (who had a dull face, little hair and no charm). The fact that he was not the time-and-motion man, reflected Hervey, as he left his study and went into the hall, was the basis of both his success and his failure.

On the stairs, Hervey met his wife. She was carrying

gardening gloves, an electric light bulb and a Bible; she too had clearly committed some error of planning. The activities indicated by these objects were all separately appropriate to a Sunday afternoon; but, presented together, they gave an impression of aimlessness, of lack of focus. Cynthia Whale was indeed likely to leave the gardening gloves in the garden, to replace a perfectly good light bulb and to arrive late for Evensong. None of these errors were irremediable, but one felt that over the years, they must be straining the stabilizing mechanism of the mind. Cynthia had always been scatty; friends waited with interest to see how soon she would become dotty. At the moment, she was well ahead of the game.

'Will you be taking your shorts to Germany?' she asked. Hervey was flying to a tariff equalization conference in Berlin next week.

'I think not. Hardly suitable for the North Sea in October.'

'Oh, it's the *North* Sea, is it? I won't bother to get them washed then.'

'I'm just going up to get the key for the filing cabinet. I think it's in my tweed coat.'

'Well it was. But I put it somewhere else when I gave the coat to Mrs Stokes to brush. I'm not sure quite where.'

'It's rather important. I want to finish my speech.'

'Yes, I see. If I knew where I put it, I'd get it for you, straight away. But as I don't I can't. Perhaps if you hadn't left it in that coat, which I told you I was giving to Mrs Stokes —'

'Perhaps if you'd asked me what I wanted done with the key and not put it in some ingenious hiding place.'

They stood on the stairs arguing gently, Cynthia a step or

two higher than Hervey, like some interminable crosstalk scene in a school production of Shakespeare. Both Cynthia and Hervey had so slight a hold on reality, so little sensual fierceness, that their quarrels in which fairly bitter words might be exchanged never left lasting scars. On the other hand, their reconciliations never brought them very close – at any rate no closer than either of them wished. They were both so contentedly self-absorbed that they found it difficult and embarrassing to make emotional contact, just as very fat people may find physical difficulties in making love. Their inflated egos rubbed against each other. But no damage was apparently done, though the friction occasionally irritated.

George, passing through the hall below, saw his parents talking at the top of the stairs. Their attitudes – his father slowly beating the air with his left hand, his mother's right arm across her breast with the hand resting on the left shoulder like a cockeyed epaulette – were to him infinitely familiar. Thus the manner of their encounter was in his eyes as stylized as that of any Byzantine madonna. The clothes, the gestures, the voices had been so often repeated that they seemed timeless. They were the conventional actor's masks which served merely as vehicles to express any emotion, any allegory.

It was fine when one could regard one's parents in that detached spirit. But that was rare. Usually they were everywhere; outside him trying to get inside him, criticizing his appearance, remoulding his temperament, straightening his tie. As their character and physique were also inside him struggling to find full expression in the perfect man, the grown George Whale, each anxiously loving parental stricture was, as is usual with parents, a combination of anxiously loving self-criticism and cheerfully unfettered abuse of the other parent. George felt himself copying Cynthia's trick of emphasizing unimportant words in a long sentence and Hervey's habit of leaning on the mantelpiece in a Gerald Du Maurier manner. He also occasionally lapsed into Cynthia's solipsist state in which the evidence of his senses seemed blurred and trivial. He even felt Hervey's lack of vigorous response to moral challenges creeping over him. This was indeed George Whale's main problem.

Six years earlier, when George was twenty-one, he had been asked for his opinion on syndicalism. He said with absent-minded sententiousness: 'I have no opinions.' He then discovered this to be true. Perhaps he thought integrity might be the thing. Merely to exist honestly had a certain stark glamour. Besides, the Sartrean wave had left one or two brackish rock-pools on the bare intellectual beaches of Winkhill; a Colonel's daughter who lived half a mile away admired Simone de Beauvoir. She and her friends spoke highly of intellectual integrity.

George had asked Ray's father, Jacob Stettin, who had been born in Prague, was a Professor of Fine Art and might be expected to know about such things, what he thought of Sartre. Jacob said Sartre was intellectually dishonest. So, George thought, where were you?

You ought perhaps to be expressing your passions freely and without constraint. Lying blissful in the long grass, heedless of autumnal mists and knobby fir cones underneath you. Ray and Annabel had at any rate shown that there was more to life than comfort.

Did Ray love her? George hoped so, though it was unlikely given Ray's restless – and successful – way with girls.

But George was a sentimentalist. He hoped he might be

able to believe in love, the love of a good, or even a bad women. What would such an event entail? George was hard-pressed to say. But he was rather looking forward to it. Yes, love might be the thing.

Chapter 2

' It may not be much of a party, I'm afraid. Fred doesn't bother about who comes or drink or anything. He really just likes noise,' said Ray.

' That doesn't say much for you asking me to come with you,' said George. ' I suppose you thought this was the only sort of party I would be allowed into.'

' Of course. There are three kinds of party – parties you can take anyone to, parties to which you can take some selected people if you ring up first, and parties which you can't take anyone to and you're pretty lucky if you can get in yourself. This is the first type.'

' I see.'

George was sitting with Annabel Meyer, more panda-like than ever, in the back seat of Ray's Jaguar. In the front seats were Ray and Gussi Ackerdorf, a cousin of the Stettins. They had just come from a bad dinner in an Italian restaurant.

' All Jewish families,' Ray had explained on the telephone, ' have an eighteen-year-old female cousin in Vienna who is coming to London for a few months to learn about English life and literature. In the same way all Jewish families have an uncle in South Africa, who may leave one a great deal of money or, on the other hand, may be put in gaol as a Communist agitator. Either way, he's rather an addition to one's life. The girl cousin is invariably a dead loss. Gussi's a great example of the genre.'

She was. Her pretty face and long chestnut hair, de-pigtailed only as a concession to English fashion, surmounted an exuberant body. George noticed a war of nerves between her muscular bust and the cross-strings which held her Austrian costume together. The bust appeared gradually to be gaining the upper hand. The flounces of her skirt emphasized her broad hips just as her openwork stockings drew attention to her powerful legs. The total effect was overwhelming but not unattractive, like a fine drayhorse covered with rosettes and horsebrasses.

It was her conversation which had united Ray and George in that life-enhancing camaraderie of dislike. She combined social and moral snobbishness with an arch inconsequentiality which she had been educated to believe must melt cold, logical masculine hearts.

' This party, it will be very grand ?'

' No, I expect it will be full of a lot of middle class painters and proletarian advertising men,' said Ray.

' Ah, Raymond, you English are so snobby. In Austria, we have now no class structure. All are simply citizens, the nobility is illegal.'

' How nice.'

' Even the Prinzessin Lange-Schwarzenhoff calls herself simply Frau Schwarz. She has two palaces and nearly twenty servants. Is that not democratic ?'

' Very.'

' But if I say to George's pappi, not " Hello, Lord Whale," but " Hello, Mr Whale," he would not be amused.

He would kick me out of the house, yes?'

'He might easily,' said Ray. 'Mr Whale is a man of quick temper.'

'I see his picture in the paper. He is a fine-looking man. George also is fine-looking but not so fine-looking as Lord Whale. In Austria, we would call Lord Whale "*ein hübscher Kerl*." '

'Would you indeed.'

'The English language is so difficult,' said Gussi with a sigh, as if she had stumbled on some hidden truth which rendered all further speech futile. But her loss of heart was only momentary.

'I think it is horrible that in England you can buy things to stop babies in the shops. You go into pharmacy and say "I want a thing to stop a baby". In Austria you cannot get such things.'

'Have you tried?'

'Certainly not. Viennese girls do not need these things.'

'What an extraordinary country it must be,' said George.

'In Vienna well-born girls are good. They do not do bad things. In England it is different, they say.'

'We live in hope,' said Ray, as he parked the car outside a sombre house off Chelsea Embankment where the party was to be held.

Ray led the way into the hall which smelled quietly of curry – the legacy of an Indian restaurant which had recently operated in the basement. The worn carpet and the awkward design of the stairs symbolized the lack of love expended on the house in the century since its speculative builder had laid the first inadequate foundations. Few had lodged in it for more than a year or two; none had wanted to do so. The house's landlords had been as transient as its inhabitants. They were sad, detached figures not like the

25

proud malevolent landladies of a genuine boarding-house. Mr Karopoulos, the present landlord, was typical of his predecessors. A tired little man in carpet slippers, he padded dutifully around his property in the hope of detecting immoral behaviour or irresponsible use of the hot water system. At this moment, he was standing outside the door of his flat on the ground floor.

' You will not make too much noise? I have respectable tenants. They must go to business early in the morning.'

' We too are respectable,' said George.

' You will not dance?' said Mr Karopoulos hopefully as if referring to some disgusting and probably illegal rite.

' Only very quietly, in our bare feet,' promised Ray.

As they climbed the stairs to the fourth floor, it became clear that Mr Karopoulos' hope was in vain. The sound of native rhythm beat down through the thin ceilings. Dancing was undeniably in progress.

The party was in a large, dark, low-ceilinged room. The room was so gloomy that though there were about fifty people dancing or talking in it, they were all huddled together along the walls. The centre of the room was empty. In one corner a gramophone was playing Ray Charles. Two thin young men stood by the gramophone intently reading the record sleeves. Several guests in black tights and of indeterminate sex were sitting on the floor. Through the melancholy howl of ' Georgia on my mind ' there came the unmistakable sound of people not enjoying themselves.

At a table near the door a spotty clergyman with fair hair was pouring red wine into some dirty glasses. He looked up and greeted George and the others.

' I'm awfully sorry to crash your party like this,' said George, ' but Ray –'

' Oh that's all right, old boy, I don't mind who crashes

my " piss-ups " as long as there's enough piss left for me.'

Evidently a hard-drinking padré with no nonsense about him, thought George. How odd that Ray had not warned him that Fred was in Holy orders. Ray wriggled past George and embraced the clergyman affectionately.

' Well, how's the ad game going?'

Fred roared with laughter and said it was pissing along and asked if Ray had heard any good ones lately. Ray said yes but nothing that was fit for mixed company. Fred roared with laughter again and said that what they all needed was a drink. As they picked their way over the sullen under-world on the floor, Fred said to George :

' I hope you don't mind this kit?'

' Good Lord, no.'

' Great. Only a couple of girls – Papists – said I'd gone too far. I say, you're not a Catholic by any chance, are you?'

' Far from it.'

' Good. I rather like this gear. Livens things up a bit, if you know what I mean.'

Fred poured out drinks and moved off. George found himself left with the two girls. Ray, with his habitual social ease and speed, was already in another part of the room.

' Do you like this sort of party?' George asked Annabel.

' Oh yes,' she replied with an earnest blink of her panda eyes. ' I mean they're my crowd. There isn't anything else, is there?'

' No, I suppose not,' said George, impressed by this ex-clusiveness.

' I mean, they may be creeps, some of them, but they do live. And you have to live, to try it all, before you get old and fat. I'd hate to get old and fat.'

' What do you mean exactly, " live " ?'

' Well, I suppose sex and jazz and all that bit. I mean you've got to have your values. I wouldn't sleep with any man I met for the first time. And I don't go much for pot. But you must have a bit of a ball before you settle down with some old stockbroker and have seven squalling kids and that, I mean, you've got to see it all before you can kick it. That's what it's all about, isn't it?'

Annabel pushed her hair back with a gesture that was nervous and yet indicated her certainty that this credo was the right one, until age and marriage should overtake her.

' But that is silly. You need not be naughty to have fun,' said Gussi from behind George's right ear, ' you can enjoy yourself without doing what you shouldn't. A few glasses of wine, a waltz and I'm happy – just like that.' She snapped her fingers dramatically, before continuing with the confident slowness of the born non-raconteur – ' I will tell you a very funny story. Once when I was sixteen we went to the Wörthersee for our holidays, and there was a very gay girl, always laughing, in the same hotel as me and Mutti, my mother. She lived in our street in Vienna but Mutti said she had a bad reputation and so of course I did not speak to her. And there was also this man in the hotel who was not at all well born. And my Mutti said it will end badly. And the girl had a baby which was born dead and the man – he was not respectable – had to go to South America. So, you see, you must not overstep the mark or you must pay for your fun.'

Annabel was dumbfounded by this grim little tale or rather by the moral bias Gussi gave it, which stood for most of what Annabel had evidently rejected. While Gussi had merely dismissed Annabel's theories as silly, Gussi's attitudes seemed to Annabel fascinating and extraordinary. That anyone of her generation could cling and cling with relish to the taboos and hypocrisies of her parents was to her incomprehensible. But having by her rejection of all that nonsense moved into the sphere of conscious moral decisions, Annabel also found Gussi an interesting study. Was there not perhaps something of value to be salvaged from Gussi's moral world – some principle which if not intellectually honest might at least help in the struggle for Life? After all, if one was to be a harbinger of the life force, any help to keep one's engine running smoothly should be welcomed.

The party had by now slowed down appreciably. The initial stimulus provided by the juxtaposition of strangers had passed off. So had the supplementary stimulus of warmth and heat and noise. People were now seriously thinking about getting girls, getting drunk or getting home or a combination of all three. The problems raised by these objectives occupied everyone's mind to the exclusion of gaiety. New talent was clearly needed if the party was to remain lively.

At this moment new talent appeared. The door swung open to reveal a short, fat ginger-bearded man of about thirty-five wearing a crash helmet and a leather lacket. He was followed by a tall, thin young man carrying a guitar. Bringing up the rear was a dark girl with a fringe. She was wearing a gipsy costume. The trio as a whole gave the impression of a troupe of wandering players, such as Victorian writers used to encounter in the Tyrol. The girl would bring out her castanets and would dance to the singing and playing of the tall man. The other might be an acrobat, the crash helmet being a modern safety precaution required by law for backward somersaults.

' Terrible time getting here,' said the ginger-bearded man

in a rich Yorkshire voice, 'the bike wouldn't start and Miriam was sick in the side-car.'

'I wouldn't have been sick if Peter hadn't tried to mess me about,' said the girl with the fringe, glaring at the tall man.

'I didn't mess you about,' said the tall man in a deep, mild voice. He was a bad painter called Peter van Aalen. Graham Earnshaw, on the other hand, was a good sculptor. His work, consisting mainly of steel sheets bolted together with few concessions to decorative appeal, was strong. His constructions had an alarming appearance of being on the move and going for you. Critics tended to retreat a step or two on entering any gallery showing his work.

The girl was Miriam Stettin, who was falling out of love with Peter van Aalen.

'I brought my guitar,' said Peter to Fred, who had now come forward, dog-collar askew, to absorb them into the party. Peter spoke mournfully as if the fact could be of interest to no one but himself. But there was only one possible outcome.

'That's great,' said Fred flatly. 'We could do with a bit of a sit-down.'

Peter went and sat on a stool at the other end of the room, adjusted his guitar and waited for the audience to come into line. His metamorphosis into the star turn had a compelling, dreamlike quality. Even those who, like George, disliked guitars and their players, soon found themselves squatting uncomfortably on the floor. Miriam had taken up a position of honour beneath the guitar, like a favourite dog at the feet of an entombed crusader. The scene was set. The Pied Piper of Hamlin could not have managed it quicker. A few unrelated chords, to indicate both versatility and the technical difficulties to be overcome, and Peter was away.

His repertoire was varied. He sang a Yiddish love song, he sang a patter number 'Le roi est à Versailles', he sang 'Zwei Matrosen aus Shanghai', he played some Bach which he had arranged for the guitar, he sang a dirty Glaswegian ballad called 'Wee Maggie fra Campbelltoun'. He then sang 'Careless Love', a request from a medical student in paint-stained jeans. During a *pianissimo* passage in this, Fred's strident voice was heard at the back of the room:

'So I said to him, look here, I don't care if we handle your campaign or not. It's a piddling little job, anyway. But if ' – The chords swelled, Peter's light tenor voice soared over all.

The audience was relaxed, they were in the hollow of Peter's sensitive hand. He paused, his fingers running idly over the strings. He let go of the audience for a moment, only to grip them more tightly.

> 'Where have all the flowers gone?
>   Long time passing.
> Where have all the flowers gone?
>   Long time ago.'

> 'Where have all the flowers gone?
>   Gone to sweethearts every one,
> When will they ever learn?
>   When will they ever learn?'

Chorus (in which the whole room joined, quietly, reflectively).

> 'Where have all the sweethearts gone?
>   Gone to soldiers every one.
> When will they ever learn?
>   When will they ever learn?'

Chorus (more strongly now).

> ' Where have all the soldiers gone?
> Gone to graveyards every one.
> When will they ever learn?
> When will they ever learn?'

Chorus (exultant).

> ' Where have all the graveyards gone?
> Gone to flowers every one.
> When will they ever learn?
> When will they ever learn?'

Chorus (elegiac, *diminuendo*).

Miriam liked the song. It expressed clearly what she felt without splitting hairs. That was the trouble with Jewish life in England; there was so much arguing, so much scoring of debating points, so much sitting in stuffy flats sharpening your mind. The elemental surge of feeling was kept too rigidly under control. Facts were disciplined and drilled like an army whereas they ought to be just a basis for the enrichment of your personality, the enlarging of your vision. Feeling was, as Goethe said, everything.

That was why she had liked Peter so much. He was a release from the rationalist prison of the Winkhill family circle. Peter never argued, never tried to trap you into contradiction. He just painted and played the guitar and made love; he had a decent private income; he was totally natural, even if his vitality was a bit low. When faced with a challenge, his body relaxed, a curtain of detachment came down over his large brown eyes, and he waited for the challenge to go away. It usually did, leaving Peter in a rather stronger position.

Miriam had, however, stayed around too long. She was beginning to irritate him like a speck of grit inside the shell. She was too ardent, too enthusiastic, too embarrassingly vital. Far from recharging his batteries, she seemed to be draining current off from him. Perhaps she was devouring him, as women were said to do.

'Who's that next to Segovia?' said George to Ray at the end of the recital.

'Oh that. That's Miriam. My sister. She's been shacking up with Peter in Notting Hill, but I think it's coming to an end soon. Come and talk to her.'

Miriam got up and rested her hand on Peter's shoulder as he put the guitar back into its case.

'You were playing well tonight.'

'You bugged me sitting there,' said Peter in the level voice which he used for being rude.

'Oh did I?'

'Yes.'

'I'm sorry.'

Peter got up and turned away to put his guitar in the hall outside.

'Hullo Miriam,' said Ray, 'this is George Whale. You remember.'

'Oh, hullo. Yes. I haven't seen you for years. How are you?'

'Very well,' said George. 'This is a great party.'

'It is, isn't it?'

Graham Earnshaw came bustling up, his leather jacket creaking.

'Have you got a fag, love?'

Miriam produced a packet of *gauloises*. Graham took

one, lit it, puffed powerfully twice in George's face and said:

'Who are you then? Haven't seen you around before.'

'This is George Whale,' said Miriam.

'Pleased to meet you, lad. I'm Graham Earnshaw. I'm a sculptor. What are you?'

'Oh, I work in a merchant bank.'

'Do you now? There must be good money in that.'

'Not really. You don't get much to begin with.'

'What do you get?'

'Only eleven hundred a year,' said George deprecatingly.

'It's not a lot for turning up at nine every morning on the dot. Still I suppose it's like an apprenticeship. Better than art school, anyway, they don't pay you at all there. Did you know that?'

'More or less.'

'We had terrible times at college. Not a penny to our names, sometimes. I said to this professor – dried-up little chap he was – why don't you get the Council to put up our grants? And this professor bloke said, " Earnshaw," Graham put on a squeaky donnish voice, " you may not make a sculptor but by gum, you'll make money." And I have, you know. Over three thousand last year, clear of tax. Better than merchant banking any day.'

'It sounds like it,' said George.

'And I'm a good sculptor too. Heavy, solid stuff – that's what I like. None of your pretty little Chadwicks and Armitages. You need a lorry to shift my stuff. And it hits you, smack in the eye, too. Here, listen to this,' – Graham took a dog-eared press-cutting out of his pocket – ' " Mr Earnshaw uses metal with a feeling of tensile strength rarely found in British sculpture today. The suggestion of outward-spiralling force, destructive in its implications, is almost

Nietzschean." I like that " almost ".'

Fred passed by, dog-collar now hanging loose. He was carrying a bottle of red wine and refilling glasses. He had the air of officiating at a Communion service that had got out of hand. Graham thrust out his glass for a refill, drained it, picked up his crash helmet from the mantelpiece, and said :

' Well I must be saying bye-bye now. Thanks very much for a lovely party, Fred. Nice to have met you, George. Can I give you a lift, love?'

' No thank you. I've had enough of your wall of death for one evening.'

' All right then. Good night all.'

George and Miriam were left together. They had been standing next to each other for half an hour, but what with one thing and another, had not exchanged a word since being introduced.

Peter van Aalen put his head round the door and announced in a loud voice to no one in particular. ' I'm off, Graham's giving me a lift.'

' That, I suppose, is that,' said Miriam. George hoped she was not going to cry. She did not.

' Would you mind if we went outside? It's too hot in here.'

' What a good idea.'

They went out and crossed the road and leant on the Embankment parapet. It was a fine night, a light wind just ruffling the trees in Battersea Park across the river. The light from a street lamp caught Miriam's face as she looked upstream at the illuminated Albert Bridge. Her eyes were shining, not with tears but with the coolness of the night air. Her face was alert, anticipatory. She did not look like a woman deserted by her lover. She looked like someone

35

arriving at an unfamiliar destination where there would be new experiences to welcome, new stimuli to respond to.

It was low tide and a narrow bank, littered with tin cans and cigarette packets, was exposed on their side of the river.

' Couldn't we get down there and walk along?' said Miriam.

' I don't see why not. There are some steps by the bridge.'

The foreshore was smelly but had a certain private charm. They walked down towards Westminster. A small stray dog appeared out of the shadows and barked gloomily at them. George picked up a tin can and threw it downstream beyond the dog who chased after it grateful for this interruption of its solitary life. At that moment, the new moon tore loose from its thin veil of cloud and revealed its startling roundness. Miriam, a yard or so ahead, turned and stopped.

' Will you kiss me?' she said.

George advanced and kissed her. She kissed warmly, hopefully, with no hint of casualness. As George held her, he too felt hopeful and pleasurably committed – more so than in many kisses preceded by much longer acquaintance.

' I should have kissed you without waiting to be asked.'

' No, girls always think of these things first. Not many are brazen enough to say so though.'

' I like brazenness. One ought to be more brazen. Perhaps you could teach me.'

' I doubt it. It just comes naturally. I always say what I feel and ask for what I want. It's common sense.'

' I suppose so. But if you don't want much, you get out of practice.'

' And if you don't feel much?'

' That's different. One calls it shyness or reticence, but it's really cowardice, fear – '

' Of being laughed at ?'

' That and other things.'

' What a worrying life you must have, George.'

' On the contrary. It's a very easy, quiet one. Too easy and quiet perhaps.'

They had reached the next set of steps to the Embankment. He helped her over the barred gate. They stood waiting for a taxi.

Inside the taxi, there was more ambitious kissing, even some fumbling with straps and zips. Nothing substantial could be accomplished in a taxi, especially one like this apparently driven by a former Grand Prix ace who turned the slightest bend into a fearsome chicane. George's stylised passes expressed not only a wish to carry the whole thing further at a later date. They presented a formal salute to Miriam's desirability.

' When can I see you again ?' said George, as they reached the large stucco Kensington house which included the Stettin flat.

' Soon. Tomorrow ?'

' Not tomorrow. I'm shooting at my grandfather's. I promised I'd go.'

' How grand. Come to supper at Winkhill on Sunday then – just Ray and me and my father.'

' That would be lovely. See you on Sunday then.'

' See you on Sunday.'

George walked home to the flat in Fulham which he shared with a University acquaintance called Humbert Stukeley. Humbert, a large, awkward young man, was reading for the Bar. At the moment he was acting as a judge's marshal on the western circuit. His absence made the flat more comfortable and stable. When Humbert was there, solid armchairs would collapse, unopened bottles would be spilt, unbreakable glasses broke.

George lit a cigarette and turned on the wireless. As usual the only station obtainable with any clarity was Radio Warsaw. The Orchestre Varsovien was playing a Chopin concerto. George conducted them energetically with his cigarette for a few bars, then poured himself a drink. He thought he really should get another job. It was very second-rate to work in a bank. One ought to do something more original.

Chapter 3

Brigadier Whale's eyes were watering. The wind blew steadily through the poplars. It was extremely cold for the first day in October. The enthusiasm with which the Brigadier had greeted the first day's pheasant shooting of the year was waning. His new weathercoat, which the man in Burberry's had assured him would be both warm and practical, was neither. The slightest breeze seemed to penetrate the porous green material, as did the dewdrops off the trees; the buttons were all in the wrong place and the coat was nipping him unpleasantly under the armpits.

It was the Brigadier's seventy-fifth birthday, a time therefore for reflection, reminiscence and stocktaking. With that self-indulgence of the imagination which characterized all the Whales, the Brigadier liked to think he had a contemplative turn of mind. The trouble was that looking back, there was so little to contemplate. Life in the trenches during the Great War which had been *the* experience in the life of his contemporaries had made little impression on him. He had only been in the front line for three weeks at a comparatively quiet time. He had then fallen on a tin helmet left in the trench by a dead NCO. He broke his arm in several places, was sent home to the envy of all and immediately developed pneumonia. He returned to active service in 1919 at Aldershot. All the other subalterns in his regiment had been killed. He had not liked any of them much, had not seen them as the flower of England's manhood. As a result of their absence, however, promotion came fast. He met the Second World War as a Brigadier and was put in charge of troop transport in the Midlands. Early in the war, one of his second cousins was killed and the Brigadier was left the Gravell Estate.

This sparse chain of experience had bred in the Brigadier a kind of optimistic determinism. He believed with reason that his own actions and capabilities were of no importance and that his fate was decided entirely by outside pressures. As he had achieved a modest success in his career, inherited a nice house and been married to a kind and pretty woman, it seemed fair to assume that he was, in a small way, one of the Elect. Given reasonably sober habits and regular attendance at church and the council, he thought that when the reveille blew for the final War Office Selection Board, the Brass Hats might well treat his application favourably.

The first pheasant of the day, an emaciated hen, got up unwillingly three hundred yards ahead. Major McCambridge, standing next to the Brigadier, removed his gun from its resting-place under his arm and pointed it into the brambles. He looked ready for anything. The hen rose more confidently and came into view. It headed for the Brigadier who fired and missed. A shot came from behind him. Colonel Strachan, a whisky-distiller who lived in the neighbourhood, had been placed as long-stop in the middle of a damp thicket in the rear. The bird fell.

The Brigadier reloaded. The day had begun badly. He wanted to relieve himself, but had been told as a child never to abandon his position during a drive. It depressed the beaters to see their efforts rendered futile by absenteeism. He wiped his nose instead, which like the bramble stems was dripping.

Major McCambridge called across to the Brigadier : ' It's the whisky that does it,' referring to Colonel Strachan's success. The Brigadier couldn't think of a reply and grinned back silently. He rather wondered why he had invited Mc-Cambridge to come and shoot. As a friend of his son Hervey, McCambridge was, he supposed, a friend of his also. Yet as far as his tired heart could dislike anyone, the Brigadier really did quite dislike Major McCambridge. The Major was short and strongly built. His face with its tough jaw, square forehead and twinkling eyes exuded health. He was a successful financier who had made his way, perhaps not quite from nothing, but from little enough to qualify as a self-made man. Altogether, Major McCambridge was clearly a flaw in the Brigadier's determinism. He was in control of things, he was affronting the fates. But perhaps, thought the Brigadier, he would be visited by the most frightful nemesis. ' Financier on £1m. fraud charge. Brigadier Whale gives evidence of good character.' That would be turning the tables neatly. On the other hand, one ought to be careful. The headlines might just as well read ' McCambridge Affair : Brigadier implicated ' or even : ' Police anxious to interview Brigadier.' Gravell House might become another Tranby Croft.

These satisfying speculations were interrupted by the appearance of a cock pheasant, passing high over him to the right. The Brigadier was slow on to the bird and his shot only ruffled the tail feathers. Colonel Strachan fired and the bird fell.

The Brigadier shivered and did up the top button of his

weathercoat; this made getting his gun into position even more difficult but it kept him warmer. With age, he found increasing difficulty in concentrating; like a man lost in a blizzard, he found it easier to detach himself from his surroundings and the problems they brought. One of these days, he thought, in a rare moment of whimsy, I'll just slip away and I won't even notice. He preferred to dream about what he was not doing rather than to make the sensual effort needed to enjoy the present. Thus, when shooting, he thought about pretty girls he had known and good food he had eaten. When being flattered by some nice young thing at dinner, he would imagine a right and left of wood-cock falling simultaneously to his gun.

The beaters drew nearer, their comforting cries could be heard in the wood with its lonely sounds of dripping and rustling. A large number of birds got up together. Several fell. George Whale, standing at the end of a line of guns, killed a distant hen hurrying away into the morning mist. A cock and hen came over the Brigadier. He brought down the hen. Colonel Strachan killed the cock. The first drive was over. Through a wall of brambles, Hatchett, the keeper, appeared, bent, wrinkled and bad-tempered, a Wiltshire Tithonus.

Suddenly, the Brigadier realized that he did not know where the only bird he had shot had fallen, that Colonel Strachan was bound to know and would by now have quietly added it to his own bag. He looked into the brambles but could see nothing. Hatchett's gloomy voice interrupted his search:

' Is there a bird down there, sir?'

' Yes, Hatchett, a hen, stone dead.'

' Them stone dead birds run a long way sometimes,' said Hatchett, smirking at the pungency of his insult. He sent his retriever into the sodden undergrowth. The retriever showed no enthusiasm for the project. Hatchett thrashed a little bush with his stick. The Brigadier parted a few brambles with his foot. The pheasant appeared to have vanished.

A large figure came up out of the mist carrying a quantity of game. Colonel Strachan threw a bedraggled hen into the bed of nettles in which the group of searchers were standing.

'That's yours, Whale. Winged bird – tried to make a run for it down the stream. Slugg caught it.'

Slugg, a large dog of indeterminate species, was still shaking the muddy water out of his coat, spattering the Brigadier as he did so. Hatchett muttered: 'Stone dead indeed,' and gave an improbably high hoot of laughter.

The other guns now appeared – those who had shot well bearing their victims before them like religious offerings, others, more discreet about their achievements, dangling them at their sides. General discussions of events so far got under way. Modesty was the keynote of the conversation.

'Guns this way please,' Hatchett shouted, and the six men in plus-fours, suddenly reawakened to their privileged status, shambled after him down the path. The beaters stood in a large happy group and cigarettes were passed round. An occasional burst of laughter from them pursued the guns through the wood. Each of the latter felt secretly that the laughter might be directed at him.

At the gate leading out of the wood, the six men paired off in twos in order to put up a barrier of conversation against the unfamiliar country silence. In this re-shuffle George drew Major McCambridge.

'Good stand that, George. Plenty of birds.'

'Yes, there were.'

' Came a bit too fast for the Brigadier, some of them.'

' Yes, I suppose he's not as quick as he used to be.'

' Do you manage to get down here much now, George?'

' A certain amount.'

' How are you keeping body and soul together at the moment?' Major McCambridge's questions came in a steady flow. As with examination papers, it was in the end better to answer one at length than to answer them all in monosyllables.

' I'm working for a newish merchant bank, Grainger Le Mercier, you probably know about them. Most of my work is background research on firms. A certain amount of figures too. You know, work it out on the slide-rule – get it wrong – add it up yourself – still wrong – give it to one of the clerks who does it in his head.'

' What do they pay you?' asked Major McCambridge alertly.

' Very little.'

' Do you find your work rewarding?' asked Major Mc-Cambridge even more alertly.

' Not very. I was told it was going to become more entertaining when I started working with the partners, making decisions and so on. I do some of that now. But the decisions I am allowed to take are just as boring as the spadework needed to take them. It's responsibility without interest, in fact.'

' I see,' said McCambridge. ' Not enough scope for a bright lad like you.' The Major's lips pursed, his forehead furrowed, his twinkling eyes narrowed. He was thinking. He was thinking indeed of some alternative job for George. His schemes were usually original; for example, one idea had been to smuggle over some poppy seed from Belgium and produce cut-price Flanders poppies under glass for the Albert Hall Festival of Remembrance. His enthusiasm passed quickly, however, and once rejected, his schemes were not regretted or remembered even if they did later succeed in bolder hands. His new idea was not startling.

' Why don't you try advertising? I've got an interest in a firm that makes films for television – a small concern, rather fun to work for. It's called Skreenjingles. They are looking for a young man who doesn't know much about the technical side but knows his way around. Might be rather valuable as experience – you could pick up a lot about the advertising game, with your knowledge of the City, you could be useful to them. Of course, I can't guarantee anything but it might be worth a go. I can certainly get you an interview with the people who run the show.'

He looked up at George with an appealing expression as if he not George was looking for a new job. Major McCambridge's urge to sell anything he could lay his hands on – people, ideas, things – had after all been the foundation of his success.

George said how kind it was of Major McCambridge to suggest it. The whole thing obviously needed a good deal of thinking over and he would give it a good deal of thinking over. This was George's normal defence against the intrusion of new possibilities into his world. If one parried the intruder's blows long enough, one was usually left in peace. What might have been called ' funk ' in a more free-spoken circle than that of his family, George preferred to see as a sort of sensitivity to life. Just as a sensitive art critic might feel degraded by a bad picture, so George found himself life-diminished by humiliating or pointless experiences; that being so, the thing to do was to nip out of the way when you saw that sort of thing looming.

The advertising game was a case in point. No other

human occupation so neatly combined the dishonest and the second-rate. At the same time, it had a spurious respectability, not allowed to bookmakers or pimps – both service industries just as necessary to the community and no more distasteful. This hard won respectability encouraged admen to think well of themselves – in itself another setback in the human struggle for intellectual and moral progress.

On the other hand, advertising did have a certain brashness, an ulcer-inducing pace. It was what George called a 'striped-shirt' industry. That is to say, one run by sharp young men skilled only in the art of persuasion and industrious only in the pursuit of high wages and short hours. These artful dodgers in television, public relations, pop music and other fields whose very nature was cloaked in jargon, managed to remove a large quantity of money from those who had spent their life in hard work and the acquisition of technical skill. Yet surely this was right. After all, it was the use of language, complex, glowing, inflected, beautiful, which distinguished man from other species. Animals might be able to communicate desire, hunger, fear or joy, but they could not discuss the significance of C. P. Snow or explain how babies were born. The highest science was that of language; the philosopher and theologian now as always were concerned with the meaning and use of words. The air was thick with the defining of terms. And if the highest science was the science of language, then the most vital technology (vital for Britain's survival as a great trading nation, vital for the world's survival in the cosmos) was the technology of language. And what was this technology but the manipulation of meaning for profit and power – that skill practised so well by Talleyrand and P. T. Barnum? As Jonathan Wild pointed out, this was what distinguished true greatness.

The path left the edge of the wood and started to climb up to the far corner of the meadow in front, where Hatchett was leaning sardonically on his stick watching the party's laboured progress up the steepish slope. Colonel Strachan stopped once or twice to admire the view of the downs which opened out beyond and below the wood. He was puffing slightly. When the top of the meadow was reached, the Brigadier allotted the positions for the next drive and the guns started to string out along the fence. This meant a re-shuffle, enabling those who had run out of conversation to repeat their remarks to new listeners. George walked beside the Brigadier.

'Major McCambridge says I might be able to get a job in a firm of his which makes advertising for television. What do you think?'

'Television? That sounds interesting, very interesting. Twenty-one million people watch television every day, you know. Must be money in it somewhere. But don't let me influence your decision – not that I could if I wanted to of course.'

The Brigadier liked being on the spot except that it seemed to require a lot of running to stay on it. His weapon was his directorship of a local plastics firm which was small but go-ahead. An industrialist who had just moved into the neighbourhood acquired the directorship for the Brigadier in return for friendship. The Brigadier never missed a Board meeting, mainly because of the large lunch which invariably, and the tour of the works which frequently, followed. He liked the works, the men on the floor were so nice and friendly.

'Just been down to the works,' he would say on his return, 'they've got the new binary blasting process installed now. Old Alf, the foreman, says it's a devil to operate. Twist

47

your balls off as soon as look at you, he says it would.'

The Brigadier and George parted to go to their respective positions. George was still pondering the career question. Though his grandfather's advice was as anodyne as his mind, it might be on the right lines. If he went into advertising he would be entering a vibrant, growing profession. Its brashness might overcome the devitalizing influence of his upbringing and environment. Fresh, unashamedly vulgar colleagues would throng into his life, enriching it, humanizing it. He might have difficulty in finding his feet at first but it would be worth it. And he could always get out again if this expedition into *terra incognita* should fail. He would ask Major McCambridge to get him an interview with Skreenjingles.

After three more drives had added little to the bag, the mist cleared and the sun shone. A rolling, dipping prospect of plain unfolded. The downland turf, a dull green after the long dry summer of that year, was occasionally patched by dark-gold fields of stubble and the first autumnal oblongs of plough. In the middle distance, the main road bounded energetically over the hills on his way to Sarum. Beyond lay the erratic shanty-town of military encampment. As at Winkhill, the camp was perched just within the eye's reach as if to provide some permanent reminder that the country of one's youth is not as open or unoccupied as it seems, that the rolling prospects are bound to shrink with age. The fates are busy with their reafforestation scheme and soon the dark encroaching armies of conifers will leave only the narrowest of rides down the middle. But the shining sun dismissed these thoughts from the minds of the shooting party reassembling for lunch. They stood at the top of the meadow and were struck by the openness of the Great Plain.

As the party walked down the track leading to the pub where lunch was waiting, the Brigadier, McCambridge and Colonel Strachan fell into line. The track was too narrow to accommodate all three. Sometimes Colonel Strachan stumbled into the wet ploughed field on one side, sometimes the Brigadier was forced up against the barbed-wire fence on the other. McCambridge pursued an unruffled course down the centre of the track. The Brigadier was ridiculously thin and bent, while Colonel Strachan's body was too massive for his matchstick legs. In between, McCambridge looked fit and well-proportioned, *Homo sapiens* between two less developed primates.

The little room in the pub was deliciously warm, a fact commented on by each new arrival. The food was unpacked by the waiting wives of Colonel Strachan and Mr Hoppington, a small, blank-faced man who was a very good shot. The guests politely jockeyed for position. Apologies were exchanged as outstretched hands failed to reach the sausage rolls and glasses of beer were removed from where they had just been put down.

A state of co-existence was eventually reached. Happy eating noises filled the room.

Slowly, appetites blunted, the guests began to talk. Both Colonel Strachan and Mr Hoppington asked George how he was keeping body and soul together. The Brigadier analysed a recent edict of the Forestry Commission which interested Major McCambridge so much that he said Mr Hoppington ought to hear it too. Mr Hoppington also thought the Brigadier's analysis interesting and told a story about his golden retriever. It went well, but the gentle laughter was drowned by the roar of hilarity from the next room where the beaters were eating.

' I expect Hatchett's at it again,' said the Brigadier, who, though loathing Hatchett, liked to build him up to his guests, as a character, an estate jester. In fact, Hatchett's interminable stories were neither funny nor, in spite of the Brigadier's implication, dirty. The successful raconteur was more likely to be Snowy Kovacs, a refugee Pole who had maintained his professionally broken English after twenty years in England, during which he had become farm foreman at Gravell. His broad face had a friendly salacious expression. His mind matched his face.

The door opened, smacking Mr Hoppington lightly in the small of the back. The sausage roll – his fifth – fell from his startled fingers, rolled into a pool of beer and lay there, winking up at him. Mr Hoppington assessed the situation quickly. There were no more sausage rolls in the basket. He leant forward to get a cigarette out of his pocket and picked the roll up with his other hand. Once more all was contentment in his corner of the room.

For the others, however, it was Snowy Kovacs who held the stage. He had entered dramatically and now stood, leaning against the doorpost, giggling.

' I am sorry to have to inform you that there's been an unfortunate accident next door, sir.'

' What do you mean, an accident?' said the Brigadier. Mrs Strachan got up and brushed crumbs off her coat; she had established a reputation locally for being a tower of strength in a crisis. When Mrs Beazley had had labour pains at a home fixture of the Gravell football club, she had been on the spot with hot water before the referee could blow his whistle; and when Percy Harris had been run over by his own tractor, she had arrived in time to turn off the ignition. But Snowy Kovacs seemed to find difficulty in replying. He merely went on giggling.

' Come on, what is it?'

'Sir, Hatchett has just slipped up in the gents and he thinks he's ruptured himself again.' The party did not immediately understand Snowy's words, which were both incoherent and thickly accented. The Brigadier was the first to decipher them and he decided that the mishap was to be treated on a serious basis.

'I suppose he won't be able to come out this afternoon, then.'

Colonel Strachan took his cue smartly and expressed sympathy.

'Poor chap, what a wretched thing to happen – especially in the middle of a good day's shooting.' As it was well known that Hatchett loathed organizing shooting-parties and never went out in the fog if he could help it, the Brigadier could hardly echo Colonel Strachan's words. But he decided to stick to the picture of the faithful retainer struck down in his happiest hour by an act of God.

Only Mr Hoppington allowed himself to find the accident funny. But his laughter was effectively muffled by the half-eaten sausage roll.

Snowy was disappointed at the lack of humorous response. Some Polish aphorism on British phlegm began to form in his mind. It was dispelled by the Brigadier's injunction that he should take charge of the afternoon's shooting. Snowy held the nominal position of under-keeper. But this was the first occasion on which he had been put in charge. His enthusiasm was so obvious and so mischievous that the Brigadier felt as if he had put a pyromaniac in charge of an ammunition dump. But the Brigadier was reluctant to countermand his order for reasons of regimental morale. So the die was cast and Snowy left the room, still chuckling.

'Who is that fellow?' said Colonel Strachan to George.

51

'Snowy Kovacs, he's a Polish refugee – manages the home farm.'

'Not often you see a Jew in the country – especially in Wiltshire,' said Colonel Strachan.

'He's not a Jew,' said George.

'Don't be deceived by his looks – you see a lot of blond Jews in Poland,' said Colonel Strachan confidently.

'When were you in Poland?' asked George, rather sharply.

'Spent three years there before the war, as military attaché. Odd thing about Jews – this love of the ghetto. Can't believe they're not still being persecuted. However well you know them, they go on treating you as an outsider, they simply refuse to be assimilated.'

George thought how consistently Colonel Strachan talked drivel on subjects he presumably knew something about. His strength was that he could never be drawn on any other subjects, out of lack of interest rather than intellectual humility.

'I can see you don't believe me, George. Well, you just wait and find out. It's a nice, warm world to be in, but all of a sudden you find yourself out on your ear; and you're just another Gentile again.'

'Cherry brandy, anyone?' Mrs Strachan's kind, weather-beaten face appeared round the door. Everyone rose and held out mugs. The cheerful atmosphere dissolved in this movement and the frowsty room was suddenly full of heavy middle-aged men with disappointed, blotchy faces. The sun went in and the warming-pans on the walls stopped gleaming. Mrs Strachan was a faded Circe in a headscarf feeding the men she had transformed into tweeded swine.

Mrs Strachan distributed the cherry brandy and sat down at George's side.

'Time for you to be thinking about getting married,' she said. This abrupt manner was common with both Harry Strachan and his wife. Yet in neither of them did it appear to be the natural expression of a laconic mind which could not be bothered with preliminaries. Perhaps they had decided on it together during their courtship as the manner most suited to their temperament and social station and stuck to it ever since, improving with practice. The listener probably gained. One felt that the Strachans' abruptness concealed two rambling minds stuffed with unorganized material.

'Well it's a question of finding the right girl, isn't it? Anyway, I'm only twenty-seven. Plenty of time.'

'Oh, they all say that then before they know it they're fat and forty and too stiff to speak to any female under fifty. I only just got Harry in time. He was on the point of scuttling back into his bachelor's shell.' She gave a curt glance of affection at Colonel Strachan who was explaining that the recession in the demand for whisky could only be temporary. George thought how odd it was that there could be even a temporary recession when one drank more each day.

'And as for finding the right girl,' said Mrs Strachan, 'it's just a matter of giving your mind to it.'

'So I've been told. It may be sentimental but I do rather like the idea of finding love without having to look for it.'

'Oh, I suppose that does happen to a few people.' Mrs Strachan implied that on the whole such people were inferior. 'But most of us have to do it by trial and error. After all, you have to pull your socks up to do anything else well. I don't see that marrying well is any exception.'

'Shoulder your muskets please, gentlemen. Back to the

53

Front,' said the Brigadier, sketching a mock salute, as he rose to his feet.

The six men went out into the clear afternoon. Mrs Strachan and Mrs Hoppington stayed behind to do the woman's work of putting the glasses, cutlery and uneaten food back into the hamper. Major McCambridge led the way looking flushed but resolute. Hobnailed boots clattered on the paved forecourt of the pub. Derry Graham, the sixth gun in the party, a bad-tempered local farmer, nearly slipped as he came out. One of the group of beaters standing around in the forecourt said, ' Whoops, there she blows,' and laughed. Major McCambridge opened his gun to make sure that it was unloaded.

' You can't be too careful, Hoppington. Slip up on these paving stones and you might get a right and left of beaters.' Mr Hoppington smiled politely.

' Ah, here comes the transport.'

A procession of vehicles drove up. The first, a cart drawn by a tractor, contained the morning's bag. Pheasants were tied in pairs to the sideboards and a dozen or so hares formed a heap of brown and white fur in one corner. The beaters jumped up on the cart and the tractor drove off up the road, the pheasants bouncing against the sideboards. Then came the Brigadier at the wheel of a Land Rover into which the six guns hoisted themselves. Finally came a gleaming black family saloon driven by Mrs Strachan. As she stopped outside the pub, two large beaters in torn khaki denims came out of the public bar supporting, indeed half-dragging the figure of Hatchett, his sharp, wrinkled face twisted with pain. The two large men were also wearing old-fashioned puttees so that the whole scene recalled some dramatic painting of the First World War representing two gallant Tommies bringing a wounded comrade back from no man's land. Hatchett entered into his part with relish. As he was bundled into the Strachan car, he paused and said:

' It's very good of you, Ma'am, to take all this trouble for a poor old man.'

' Oh do get in, Hatchett,' said Mrs Strachan in the down-to-earth tones of Nurse Cavell.

Hatchett slumped into the back seat and was driven off in state to Sarum Infirmary where his own diagnosis of recurrent rupture was confirmed.

The afternoon's shooting was to take place down in the rodbeds that stretched along the river which ran through the village of Lower Gravell. The guns lined out along one of the raised grassy paths which had been cut through the thick jungle of tall, golden-yellow rods. The rods were to be cut down next year to make way for neat plantations of poplars. As if knowing this was to be their last season the rods had grown to unprecedented heights. They resembled some crop of corn grown by giants. The beaters, fighting their way through the crackling wilderness, looked like harvest mice.

There were a few moments of complete silence. The sun was now shining brightly. George felt hot inside his tweed coat. McCambridge lit a Turkish cigarette. Mr Hoppington tapped his pipe out against a stone and moved a few yards along the path so as to be equidistant from George and Harry Strachan. The Brigadier took off his cap, smoothed down his white hair and put the cap back on again. Major McCambridge shifted from one foot to another in order not to get pins and needles. Derry Graham watched a blue-tit trying to establish a secure perch on a flimsy alder-tree.

Suddenly there was a sound of quacking and cries of ' Duck over ' from the distant beaters. A duck and drake rose almost vertically from a little pond in the middle of the rodbed and went back over the beaters. Soon the guns could see them circling high over their heads well out of shot. The hysterical quacking faded into the silence.

' Went back,' said Major McCambridge, ' wise beggars.'

Gradually the sounds of the beaters became audible – the crackling of the rods, the splashing through puddles, the stumbling over alder-stumps, the traditional cries of encouragement to the birds. Snowy Kovacs' strangled yodel formed a strong continuo to the intermittent ' Br-brr's ' and ' Ai-ai's ' of the rank and file. Eventually the beaters became visible, at first fleetingly through the rods, then with increasing clarity until they finally plodded up onto the grassy path. No birds appeared.

' It's like walking through a bloody haystack down there,' said one old man.

The Brigadier bustled along the path.

' Sorry about that. We usually have a pretty good stand down in these rodbeds, but all the birds seemed to have gone up to sun themselves on the stubble today. We'll take the Potter's Field next, I think.'

The Potter's Field was a dismal irregular piece of swamp about two hundred yards from the river, overgrown with rods, alder bushes and willows. In the middle was a medium-sized muddy pond in which a Mr Potter, deceived by his wife, had drowned himself in 1859. The historical pun on the story of Judas had added the definite article to the swamp's title. It was certainly not worth thirty pieces of silver except from the shooting point of view. The pond was at least secluded, sheltered from the frost and rich in plant and insect life. Hence there were usually quite a few duck to be picked up there and a snipe or two.

Snowy Kovacs placed the guns in a semi-circle round the

56

edge of the field just inside the fence. The rods and willows were so thick that no one could see his neighbour. Then at a signal blast from Snowy's whistle the beaters started gingerly forward from the other side of the swamp. When they were about thirty yards from the pond, the duck got up. There were about thirty of them, at first rising in a shapeless massing of whirring and quacking, quickly arranging themselves into a discernible formation. Then, their serenity only half-recovered, they came over the firing line, wheeling and gaining height all the time. Mr Hoppington got two, George and the Brigadier one each, Derry Graham winged a drake and Colonel Strachan killed a duck which fell far away on the other side of the river. The ducks who survived this Armageddon, during which the sky seemed to be full of shot and smoke and the feathers of fallen comrades, hurried on, higher and higher, turning to the south, to the waters of the Hampshire Avon where their peace would be disturbed only by unarmed courting couples from Fordingbridge.

The beaters, still invisible, resumed their advance discussing the moment of high drama that had just passed. The guns stared fixedly at the various trees and patches of rods which marked the last resting places of their prey. Without careful marking, ten duck shot down could so easily turn into two picked up.

There was a small flash of grey and white on the right of the line – a snipe. Colonel Strachan fired and missed. The snipe passed behind a couple of willows. Strachan fired again. There was a cry of pain from the willows. Major McCambridge appeared magically like a heavyweight Ariel from behind the trees, rubbing his hip and gesturing wildly with his gun. A loaded gun should not, of course, be treated in this manner.

' I'll get the man who did this! I'll sue! I'll sue!' The Major's voice rang plaintive, banshee-like across the swamp.

' My God, I am most awfully sorry,' shouted Colonel Strachan into the wind.

' What?' shouted McCambridge with the wind.

' I am most terribly sorry,' shouted Colonel Strachan.

' Sorry – is that all you can say?' shouted McCambridge, now vigorously rubbing his left buttock. ' Chap deliberately peppers me with shot and then just says he's sorry.'

' I can't apologize enough,' shouted Colonel Strachan, plunging into the swamp to go to McCambridge's aid. He got stuck in a boggy patch and left one of his boots behind in his frenzy of contrition.

' I should think not,' said McCambridge as the massive one-booted figure struggled through the rods. ' Luckily just a flesh wound but I might easily have been paralysed. This isn't a damned shooting-range, you know.'

McCambridge, most of his wrath spent, consented to be led by Strachan to the Land Rover at the far end of the Potter's Field. His mind was, however, evidently still dwelling on the idea of legal action and the prospect of huge damages, for he said as he was being driven off to the doctor to have his wounds dressed :

' You wouldn't have a leg to stand on in court, you know, Strachan. Not a leg to stand on.'

The rest of the party, a little shaken by the incident, stood waiting for further instructions from the Brigadier.

' I think we might pack it in for the afternoon, now that Jack and Harry aren't here. What I can't understand is why Jack came to be standing behind those willows at all. He should have been thirty yards back just inside the fence like the rest of us. That idiot Snowy must have made a balls up.' But when questioned, Snowy protested innocence. He had placed the Major in the correct position. Was it not, however, possible that the Major had crept forward in order to get at the duck when they came over? Might it not in fact have been the Major's own fault that he had been peppered? It might even be taken as a just piece of retribution for the Major's attempt to improve his own sport at the expense of the others.

This ingenious line of reasoning had to remain unproven, as it was later strongly denied by McCambridge. But Snowy's evidence could not be quite disregarded as McCambridge was extremely evasive about whether he had stayed in the position he had been put.

'Not exactly. No, I wouldn't say exactly the same position.'

Further questioning was impossible outside a court of law and nobody except McCambridge had any inclination to take it that far. One thing only was certain; the Potter's Field had claimed its second victim.

Chapter 4

George Whale came down from London by one of those empty Sunday trains which as a concession to the day of rest seemed reluctant to reach their destination in anything but the longest time possible. The forty minutes it normally took to reach Winkhill were extended into seventy. George was not based on Winkhill for the week-end because Hervey had gone off to his tariff equalization conference in Berlin and Cynthia had gone off to stay near Haywards Heath with a friend, a widow rather older than herself whom nobody else ever saw. Cynthia referred to her as ' Poor Evelyn '. Beyond that, nothing was known of her. As a result of these movements, Larchmount had temporarily closed down for visitors.

The Sunday papers littered the carriage. George sat in a sea of comment designed to flatter and confirm every shade of opinion, features to stimulate every emotion with a little news floating on the surface. Sex, money, religion, gracious living – all were briskly dealt with, their secrets laid bare with a flick of the scalpel. George generally read the business pages. This was as a result of a tip from Evan Pratt, a clever Welshman with Trotskyite inclinations who worked in George's bank. ' When you first come here, boy,' said Evan, gripping George urgently by the elbow, ' they don't tell you anything, but they expect you to know about every bloody deal that's in the air. You just read the Sunday papers, boy, the Sunday Editors spend the whole week listening to drunken gossip in *Short's* bar. They put most of it in the papers. And it all turns out to be bloody true.' Evan's advice was good. Every time George was summoned to see his boss and charged with some research for a possible, mark you only possible, and highly confidential deal, he already knew the answer.

George had unearthed this week's nugget in a little city gossip column called ' Going Shares '. It read :

' I hear that H. & J. Thwaite, an old-established Durham floor-polish firm may be due for a spring-clean! A merger with the American giant Associated Detergents is strongly rumoured. Wielding the mop : Grainger Le Mercier, the go-ahead merchant bankers. Thwaite shares should rocket.'

There it was, his work for the week, plainly advertised like some forthcoming event of national importance. On Monday, Timmy Le Mercier would ask him to examine the balance sheets of Thwaite's for the past ten years. He would also be asked to have a look at the distribution system, the retail outlets and, if possible, the directors – their reputation, previous experience and their drinking habits, and sexual aberrations insofar as these affected their health and capacity for business. On Thursday George would present this detailed monograph containing everything one wanted to know about Thwaite's and quite a lot besides. On Friday, Le Mercier would report that the representatives of the American firm were ' very happy ' with George's work. On the following Monday, the Americans would be instructed by head office in New York that they already had enough on their plate and were not as of now ready to expand any further Britain-wise. The deal would be, vulgarly speaking, off. Such a deal, however advantageous, had little chance of coming up again in the same form, directors being on the whole shy of trying already tried new ideas. It looked as if one was losing one's touch, one's drive, even one's acumen. So George's research would become a work of the purest scholarship, quite without practical application. It would remain un-challenged, unconsulted as The Thwaite's File, until Thwaite's should hit the news again. Then some up-to-date, yet more definite material would be assembled by another of Grainger Le Mercier's bright young men. If George failed to make his mark in the bank, it might of course be George again. Not an attractive prospect.

The train eventually reached Winkhill. George tore 'Going Shares' out of the paper and put it in his wallet. He got out of the train and started up the sandy, rhododen-dron-fringed lane which led to Pontrilas, the Stettin house. Pontrilas was not the slate-roofed coal-blackened villa which its name suggested, but a small, square mansion in cream stucco with shuttered windows. A motor bicycle with a sidecar stood outside the door. Ray was leaning against the porch smoking a cigarette. He greeted George and led him round the back of the house, where they found Graham Earnshaw and Professor Stettin sitting in wicker rocking-chairs and arguing. Graham was gesticulating with his glass of whisky. 'But don't you see, Professor, all these nice liberal values of yours are dead, passé. Guernica, Auschwitz, Hungary, you can't believe in human progress after them, now can you?'

'You can believe in anything if you give your mind to it,' said Professor Stettin. 'George, how nice to see you.

Come and sit down. Ray, we all need some more to drink.'

' Now, my dear Graham, I simply do not at all see why these brutal episodes you mention should destroy my nineteenth-century optimism. Basically, I am of sanguine humour. I was believing that things would turn out all right, would indeed get better during the First World War, when I was a schoolboy in Prague, and the flower of western manhood was either being killed, or starving or mutinying against their leaders. I felt the same when I was lecturing on Caravaggio in Vienna at the time of the Anschluss. A few years later, I was giving the same lectures in California almost within earshot of Pearl Harbour. But my faith remained unshattered.'

' Of course, I'm not saying you cannot deceive yourself,' conceded Graham graciously, ' but if you're really honest with yourself, you must agree that your ideas just don't work any more. They aren't relevant.'

' Certainly they are,' said the Professor.

' Look here, to my mind it's very simple. There is only one way of being an honest bloke these days – to be totally natural, violent, to let the dark side of your nature rip. That's what I'm after.'

' I don't like your credo much,' said the Professor. ' I don't think it would suit me. The trouble about the natural man – or the monkey man as I prefer to call him – is that you need natural talent for the part. Most of us just haven't got it in us. Of course, I do see that liberation of one's urges is a good deal more enticing than their sublimation.'

At the bottom of the garden, George could just see Miriam in a sky-blue dress picking chrysanthemums. She was absorbed in her work like a figure in the background of an allegorical picture; in the foreground, satyrs carousing, in the distance, the Campagna. She collected her quota of flowers and climbed up the sinuous path to the veranda. George rose awkwardly from his chair, which creaked, and kissed her on the cheek. Graham raised his glass to her.

' I can see you're talking about Vienna, Dada,' said Miriam. ' You've got that central European look in your eyes.'

' Yes, it's one of my few remaining luxuries of sentiment,' said the Professor, drawing his hand across his face with exaggerated weariness.

' Do you long to go back?' asked George.

' Only as a tourist, certainly not as part of the university community. I am naturally an extra-mural academic. And in Vienna there is such an atmosphere of bourgeois gemüt-lichkeit, of little dinners for the faculty and their wives in overcrowded flats, of weekly visits to the opera, of Sunday afternoon expeditions to the Wienerwald. It's a world complete in its own way, but very stifling.'

Ray came out from the lounge and said that dinner was ready. The party on the veranda rose simultaneously as if royalty had suddenly appeared on the scene. Professor Stettin leaned heavily on his stick as he walked through the lounge into the dining-room. He looked much older from the back. His thin body bent over to the right as a result of years of limping and deep lines were cut in the nape of his neck. It was only his clear thin features and the animation of his expression which had managed to outflank the advance of time. The features and the animation re-appeared in Ray's face, but less fine, less strong, so that Ray looked quick rather than intelligent. In Miriam, the fineness was not so emphatic; the antennae quivered, but they were for receiving not transmitting.

The dining-room was over-furnished. It was dominated

by a large oak sideboard, which limited movement round the dining-table. Graham caught his coat on a projecting ledge of the sideboard. A silver partridge skidded a few inches across its glass top, decided not to take off and stopped, rocking slightly on its uneven feet in front of a seven-branched candlestick.

'No space, no space,' said the Professor sighing. 'When my wife left me, I was determined to clear some of the furniture out of here, but the ethos – by which I mean the smell of cooking and the memory of a hundred mediocre dinner parties – was too strong for me. So I left it as she liked it – cosy perhaps but uncomfortable.'

'Your study would make a much better dining-room,' said Miriam. This was an old routine from which nobody expected action to follow.

'True, true. But I do need space to think. One cannot be expected to master Raphael's spatial values in a cubby-hole like this. Eating, on the other hand, requires no special effort of the imagination.'

'Anyway, everyone is at their most Jewish in a dining-room,' said Ray. 'Judaism is so mixed up with gastronomic values. And you have these ghetto rules, too. You can't get into the dining-room until the gong goes and you can't get out again till everyone's finished.'

'Besides,' said Miriam, switching her tack, 'our dining-room isn't as small or as cluttered up as the Meyers', and their drawing-room's a complete desert. You see Mrs Meyer at the other end of it and you think it must be a mirage.'

'Unfortunately it never is,' said Ray. 'But you really ought to see their dining-room, George. It's like dining with the Rothschilds in the 1890's. Great wood carvings every-where and brassbound treasure chests, hideous ornate silver and Mrs Meyer's breasts swelling out of her Balenciaga dress and lowering over the food like two fleecy clouds. Real back-to-the-womb stuff.'

' You exaggerate, Ray,' said the Professor. ' Ruth Meyer was a great beauty in my youth. She's still a good-looking woman.'

' Surely a little Junoesque,' said Ray, taking another spoonful of consommé.

' Well, of course, we all liked that then. I'm afraid Central European standards of beauty rather lagged behind the Bright Young Things and their flat chests. I remember – ' A half-suppressed reminiscent smirk was spreading across the Professor's face, when his eye was caught by the bottle of horseradish sauce waiting to enliven the tasteless beef which was to follow the consommé.

' Miriam, is it totally beyond your powers to serve the horseradish in the sauce boat?'

' Couldn't find it, Dada.'

' You might just as well throw tomato ketchup on everything and be done with it. I don't ask much in the way of gracious living. Just a little trouble is all I *exige*. Simply pour the horseradish into the receptacle I have provided at some expense. That's all I ask.' The Professor's urbane voice sharpened. His fingers drummed on the table.

' Sorry, Dada, couldn't find it.'

' It's quite expensive, you know. You may think George II sauceboats grow on trees, but they don't, I promise you. What have you done with it then? Pawned it, I suppose, to pay for an abortion for one of your friends, I should think. Or perhaps for yourself. Yes, more probably yourself. That's right, you pawned my sauceboat to pay some old witch to get rid of your little van Aalen. That's it.'

The Professor's voice was shrill and ragged. He was half-way up from his chair, keeping his balance by pressing his fingers on the table. Miriam had been crying noisily and at the same time listening for the point of no return, for the insult which could not be smoothed over. It had now been delivered. She rose, folded her napkin and said, 'Would you excuse me please,' to Graham Earnshaw, whose chair was blocking the way to the door. Graham stood up and pulled his chair closer to the table, which meant he had to lean forward so that his head almost touched the Professor, who was still frozen in his semi-upright position. George was making bread pellets on his side-plate with precision and concentration. Ray was leaning back in his chair, looking at the ceiling in a detached sort of way. Miriam slammed the door behind her. It failed to shut, and Graham tiptoed across to shut it like a conscientious stage-hand during a first night.

'Would you pour us a little wine, Ray,' said the Professor. He was clearly the great actor relaxing after a demanding performance. Ray started looking for the corkscrew. 'Curious,' said the Professor, finding his feet with ease, 'how difficult it is to be nice to one's children, when one finds it such a pleasure to be agreeable to outsiders.' His tone was detached, aphoristic.

'There are certain unavoidable tensions within the – ' said Graham.

'There are indeed,' said the Professor.

'In fact,' continued Graham, ' I think family life's on the way out. I don't see how you can stop it. It's not just the war of the generations, different styles in clothes, talk and all that. It's the decline in parental authority. You learn much quicker today that your dad's not God Almighty and that your mum's a complacent old bag who stopped thinking for herself the moment the wedding bells rang out.'

67

' But,' said George, ' you do have certain things in common, shared experiences, relations and so on. You must have worked up a bit of affection for them.'

' Oh yes, we've done time together. But you don't choose your fellow-convicts. I don't see why I should sacrifice all my real friends, my sculpture and my freedom for an orgy of family reminiscence.'

' I don't see that you've done all that much sacrificing,' said Ray. Graham was wearing an expensive, if dirty, leather jacket, a pink poplin shirt and a yellow silk tie.

' Well, I got out in time, didn't I, before they consumed me.' Graham spoke with relish, his red beard wiggling like a minor prophet who had just escaped ordeal by fire.

George had listened with interest to the Professor's fancy ranging over the frontiers of human thought. At the same time he wondered whether he ought not to go and see whether Miriam was all right. Did it not show callousness, or at least a certain lack of spontaneous response to the sight of his beloved in distress that he had made no move on her behalf? She might, in fact, recover better by herself but surely there was something wrong in his sitting here and stolidly eating his crème caramel. Lovers ought to act impulsively in such situations. On the other hand, the position could be taken as an old-fashioned one in which the only lady present had left the gentlemen to their port and male conversation. There was, in fact, no port, only some sticky marsala. The Professor again complained about the low standard of catering.

' Miriam seems to think she's running a soup-kitchen.'

Ray pointed out that the Professor himself usually provided the drink. He had indeed frequently said that choosing wine was one of the few pleasures left to him.

The Professor did not reply. He got up and led the party

out on to the veranda. Miriam was sitting on the garden steps, chewing a blade of grass and looking out into the darkness. George brought her a cup of coffee and sat down beside her.

' Are you all right?'

' Yes. I'm sorry about that scene. Dada hasn't really forgiven me for leaving home and going to live with Peter. He can get rather edgy, particularly when his own comfort is threatened.'

' Don't we all,' said George tentatively.

' I know. It's too boring.'

' Still, I think your father's rather impressive. He's got a very wide range and great energy too, I should think.'

' Oh, he's with it all right. And he has moments of surprising sweetness. He suddenly does very kind things which one wouldn't expect. I suppose that's the other side of his edginess.'

Miriam took the blade of grass out of her mouth and tickled her toes with it through the straps of the sandals.

' Would you laike to see the garden? It's really quaite naice,' she said in a mock refined voice.

' I don't mind if I do.'

' All right. We'll have a midnight mystery tour then.' She got up and lazily stretched out her arms. ' We're just going for a quick walk, Dada.'

' Will you be warm enough, darling?' said the Professor.

' Don't miss the black tulips, they're particularly fine at this time of night,' said Ray.

The moon provided enough light to indicate the edges of the path, which descended steeply to a water-garden where the erratic splashing of a little waterfall could be heard faintly from the veranda. The garden ended with a pond surrounded by silver birches and clumps of azaleas, anonymous shapes in the darkness. Behind it, a white wooden fence was still visible, separating the cultivated wilderness of the garden from the cultivated wilderness of the golf-course. Beyond the fence a strip of heather ran down into the pale gulf of the bunker guarding the ninth green. George and Miriam exchanged romantic rather than sensual kisses. The moment was too ethereal, the landscape too moonlight, the air too cold for anything else. Yet George remembered, as his lips brushed Miriam's delicate cheekbone, that Ray and Annabel Meyer had not found it too cold for a roll in the heather a few days earlier. Had the temperature been a degree or two higher that day? Or was this readiness to brave the elements for love yet another criterion of vitality?

Certainly, he thought, you could not accuse Miriam of cold-bloodedness, as she burrowed restlessly into his embrace.

'You are a warm little bundle,' he said with mock-paternal indulgence.

'Well, I've got my love to keep me warm, haven't I?' she said.

'I rather think you have.'

'Darling George.'

Above them the voices of Graham Earnshaw and the Professor, thrown out from the sounding-board of the veranda, hovered in the night air like disembodied spirits. They were discussing civilization. Graham was against it.

'Henry Miller's really got something. I think we'd all be much better off if we made a bonfire of all our art, history, myths, morals – the lot – and made a fresh, vital start. Why should we be burdened with the mistakes of past generations? Why should we have to wear second-hand clothes?'

'But do we have to?' said the Professor. 'Surely the revolt of the young lions against the embattled academics is a rather outdated idea today. My contemporaries are all highly suspicious of any young man who doesn't declare all previous standards of art and morality dead. We are obsessed with the necessity of keeping up. Only the other day, Professor Callender, who can't be a day under seventy, compared Palestrina to rhythm and blues. And in my Slade lectures, I shall attempt to " hot up " Grünwald's image by pointing out his debt to Francis Bacon. Surely we old fogies can't go further than that.'

'Ah, you may be ready to accept new ideas. But you can't *feel* them. You can't get rid of your cultural shackles. What we need is a new civilization, a new freedom.'

The well-groomed silver birches shivered as Graham's voice rolled stridently down the hill. It was getting colder. George and Miriam walked arm in arm up to the lighted stage of the veranda. Ray was sitting in the rocking-chair in the corner reading a paperback. Graham was on his feet gesturing at the Professor who lay, consciously urbane, in a deck-chair.

'I am afraid I must be getting back to London. The last train goes in about ten minutes,' said George.

'Ah, yes,' said the Professor, ' clearly one must get up early to make money in the City. But don't dream of catching trains. Miriam will be driving up and can give you a lift, can't you Miriam?'

'Yes, of course, Dada.' She was irritated by this fatherly manoeuvre, particularly as she had intended the arrangement all along and so, she imagined, had George.

'That would be awfully nice,' said George flatly. Not flatly enough, however, to prevent the Professor from smiling a wise smile.

71

Graham sat twiddling a half-full glass of whisky. Evidently he was not to be moved until the nature of the cosmos had been fully defined. Ray said he was off to bed, there being a limit to the amount of metaphysical exegesis he could take. The Professor said good-bye affably to George and kissed Miriam. He expressed the hope that she would be in a better temper tomorrow. Miriam was already putting her suitcase in the car and did not hear.

The route from Pontrilas to the London road took them past the entrance to Larchmount. George suddenly remembered there was a virgin crate of whisky in the drink cupboard – a tribute from some American admirer of Hervey's statesmanship. He asked Miriam to stop the car and ran up the drive with the intention of removing a bottle or two for the flat. Miriam sat in the car fiddling with the radio.

The front door of Larchmount was ajar. As George came into the pitch-dark hall, he realized the house was not empty. Yet at the same time it was not occupied in an open, above-board way. Burglars? The front door left open for ease of getaway? It was the work of a moment for George to conceal himself behind a large oak dresser.

Someone was coming down the stairs. Clearly a stranger who was unfamiliar with the loose stair rod on the fifth step. But a stranger with fine balance who succeeded in remaining upright.

'Cynthia darling, where's the damned light switch?' George thrilled to the vibrant tones of Major McCambridge.

'At the bottom of the stairs on the left, just by the drink cupboard.' Cynthia Whale's voice floated down from her bedroom, distant but compelling like one of those voices which guided Joan of Arc to her destiny.

McCambridge found the switch and the hall became a

blaze of light. He was simply clad in a pale-blue sports shirt and matching socks. As he bent down to open the cupboard and take out a couple of cans of beer, George caught a tantalizing glimpse of his buttocks, firm and globular.

' Hurry up, angel, I'm thirsty,' Cynthia called.

' I bet it's not just for beer either,' shouted back the Major.

The voice upstairs giggled.

McCambridge shut the cupboard and loped up the stairs two at a time, pausing only to turn the light off at the top.

George left the house and tiptoed down the drive back to Miriam.

' Any luck?'

' No, the cupboard was locked and I couldn't find the key.'

' Was there someone in the house? I thought I heard voices.'

' Just me singing, I expect.'

' Do you often burst out singing?'

' Quite often. I sing very flat.'

' Rather nice all the same. Will you sing for me, now?'

George started on ' Green Grow the Rushes-O ', but without his normal brio. Miriam joined in, jerking her head from side to side in time with the song. Her window was open and the wind blew her dark hair across her cheek.

George reviewed the situation. The incident, though of course shocking, was life-enhancing. He had always thought of his mother as thin and weary, her prettiness fading into a vague bitterness. That picture would have to be repainted. Cynthia Whale was now a brittle creature, as sensual as a wild-cat and hungry for life. Hervey's embraces would have long seemed stale; Jack McCambridge, healthy and masterful, must have entered her life at the critical moment. Just how he had entered it was an interesting speculation. Had they met at some cocktail party for the Anglo-Belgian Trade Association? Had Hervey Whale been partnered with McCambridge in the Winkhill foursomes? Certainly George could not remember that McCambridge had ever come to dinner.

Then, the meeting accomplished, how had Cynthia countered the Major's unmistakable come-hithers? ' No, it's too ridiculous, I couldn't think of it.' That cool distance in her voice would surely dishearten most lovers. On the other hand, it might have spurred on the tenacious McCambridge.

And in the end, George reflected, his mother was probably a pushover. He could see her slipping with ease from ennui to the languor, the irresponsibility of sexuality. Disregarding the sanctity and the unity of the family, she would have plunged headlong into McCambridge's practised arms.

Disgusting of course it was. The fires of lust really ought to be dying down by now. But worse than the staining of her marriage bed was Cynthia's betrayal of all she so vaguely stood for. Were a thousand meetings of the Women's Institute come to this? Did regular attendance at matins mean so little? Was the combination of those fifty years of moral training so easy to crack?

Skating easily over the surface of his reactions, George suddenly crashed through a patch of thin ice. Horror and nausea rolled through his stomach like New Year revellers. George clenched his fists and pressed his spine against the car-seat. For a moment he blacked out. Gradually the tide of adrenalin receded. George relaxed, as the forces of law and order regained control of his nerve centres. But his left hand still shook as it rested on his knee – a pocket of terrorist resistance. He opened the window and gulped in fresh air. He turned to look at Miriam.

She had abandoned ' Green Grow the Rushes-O ' at the Seven who went to Heaven. She was now softly singing ' Voi che Sapete ' and flashing her headlights at slower drivers. George began stiffening his leg against an imaginary brake-pedal. Miriam noticed this and gradually increased speed, forcing George into speech.

' Awful lot of traffic on the road tonight.'

' Yes darling, we'd have to crawl along if they hadn't widened the road.'

' Rather a pity they didn't widen it properly, so one could overtake safely the whole way.'

' Oh, it's not too bad if you judge your moment,' said Miriam, as she swung out from behind a lorry which had ' wide load ' emblazoned on the back. A Jaguar shot round the corner coming the other way. The girl in the fur coat, nestling against the driver suddenly sat up, straight. She looked rather pale. Someone's tyres squealed. Miriam hooted.

' Those flashy Jag types never keep on their own side of the road,' she said.

George surrendered.

' I wonder if you wouldn't mind driving a little slower. Since my accident – '

' Oh, I'm so sorry. I didn't know you'd had a crash. Was it a bad one?'

' I was all right, just a little shaken. But the man who was giving me a lift, well he had to have his leg amputated. And he's more or less lost the sight of one eye.'

' Who was he?'

' Nobody you'd know. He was a chap I was working with, on a job for the bank up in the Midlands. He was just giving me a lift back to my hotel.' George stopped as if unable to find words to describe the horror adequately. It was a mistake to compound falsehood by too much detail.

'How awful.' said Miriam, with tender interest. The truth-value of the story was of no consequence to her, only the human factor. She slowed down substantially, as a tribute to the depth of George's experience. It was at least ten minutes before she had built up to full speed again.

The traffic thickened, the neon signs crowded in along the dual carriageway. George felt the habitual angst of Sunday evening, of the return to the uncertainties of city life to which the Great West Road provides such a grim reintroduction. Miriam turned off the main road along avenues of stucco, wistaria and parked cars. The ceremony of initiation was over and they were once again members of an ordered metropolitan society. A pillared portico every five yards, a lamp-post every ten and a policeman within call – such are the changeless ingredients of Kensington. As George and Miriam got out of the car at the Stettin's flat, only the hoarse giggles of a couple of West Indians returning from the pub suggested the lawless, brutal world on which this mercantile security was based.

'Would you like some whisky?' said Miriam, as she threw off her coat and turned to face George in the spacious drawing-room.

'Very much, but I'd like you even better,' said George advancing.

He kissed her and they slid impatiently down on to the sofa. George fumbled with the button of her white shirt, as with the string of a well-made Christmas parcel.

'Oh, George,' said Miriam, her eyes glowing. He undressed her quickly, lovingly. Major McCambridge could not have been more attentive.

Later, a whisper of tristesse passed across her face.

' George, we don't know each other very well, do we?'

' That's the charm of our relationship.'

Miriam sat up and said :

' I think you'd better go now.'

' Why, darling?'

' I just would like you to, please. I want to think.'

' Are you angry, Miriam? Do you wish – ?'

' Oh, no.' She grinned.

' Then why?'

' Please I'm very tired. I do love you, George.'

' Oh, all right.'

He picked up his trousers and put them on. He did up his shirt and put the shirt-tails inside his trousers. With his foot he fished his shoes out from under the sofa.

Miriam sat motionless on the sofa. Her clothes were still lying on the floor, except for the shirt which she had draped casually across her breasts.

' Do you really think it's a good idea, George? I mean, do you think we're suited?' George put his arm round her and kissed her. He picked up her clothes and piled them neatly at the other end of the sofa.

' Because you musn't feel committed, George. Just because – you don't have to pretend.' She started crying.

George noticed he had his trousers on the wrong way round. They were rather uncomfortable. He took them off and put them on properly.

' I'm not pretending anything,' he said.

She sniffed and smiled bravely. Pulling the shirt round her shoulders, she got up and went to get a dressing-gown. George thought how much nicer than Major McCambridge she looked from behind.

He put on his coat and walked into the hall. Miriam, thinking perhaps he was going without saying good-bye, ran

77

into his arms from the other side of the hall. They embraced with the fervour of Russians welcoming Easter Day. Love was risen indeed, fresh and lyrical, not at all like the sordid physical passions of middle age.

Chapter 5

The girl sitting opposite George uncrossed her legs. He had been reading the advertisement above her – If you want to get Ahead, get a Hat. His early-morning brain was drowsily coping with the complexities of this statement. Surely the possession of a head must be logically antecedent to the acquisition of a hat. A bowler placed midway between the shoulders would look grotesque. The Stock Exchange would be thronged with Baron Samedis. Besides, the social advancement referred to in the poster would be nullified. If none had heads and all had hats, who would be the gentlemen?

But the girl opposite was really rather attractive. Her figure was not as good as Miriam's of course; her legs were a little puffy. But she had fine, golden hair down to her shoulder and a simple, well-proportioned face shaded with kindness. On the whole, however, George thought Miriam won on points. The pull of her emotional energy outweighed, for him, any defects of feature or style, just as the fighter with the big punch could usually flatten the faultless boxer.

This survey of female talent had become a feature

of George's journey to work. The girls sitting or standing with George in the Tube were handicapped. With their dry skins, their sleep-encrusted eyes and their untidy lipstick they could not hope to compete with Miriam still lying warm and lustrous in George's bed in Fulham.

She had been staying with George for about a week. Humbert Stukeley, George's co-tenant, was acting as a judge's marshal somewhere in Wales. His bedroom alone in the flat preserved its cold air of bachelor rectitude – silver-mounted hairbrushes and studboxes symmetrically arrayed on the dressing-table, thick suits in the hanging-cupboard, thick lawbooks in the book-case.

Elsewhere misrule reigned. The bathroom had suddenly become full of Miriam's underclothes and little pieces of paper with telephone numbers on them. Apples and apple-cores were scattered all over the bedroom. The cores came to predominate. Books were everywhere, open, half-open and standing on their spines, serving as table-mats for glasses. Cigarette-ash and cigarette stubs seemed to cover every available surface like the scumble of an old master.

George found the disorder pleasantly symbolic of the change in his inner life. For Miriam, it was the execution of an important principle, her need to combat the bourgeois obsession with tidiness and cleanliness, to vindicate gloriously the way of freedom and art and personality development and existential self-justification – in short, the need to live.

The arrival of Mrs Goodenough, the daily woman, at half past eleven four mornings a week, provided Miriam with an opponent. In order to set up a fully Manichean situation, Miriam had to stay in bed dropping cigarette-ash over the sheets and drinking black coffee. She really preferred getting up early, especially as the bedclothes were

covered with knobbly crumbs from the breakfast that
George had lovingly brought her.

But Mrs Goodenough was worth these minor discomforts.
Gaunt, varicose-veined, strict Baptist, supporting unaided
a drunken husband and an ailing daughter, she disapproved
of Miriam for reasons as much hygienic as moral. Mrs
Goodenough passed through the bohemian splendour of
George's bedroom only in order to clean Humbert's room.
As the untidiness everywhere else seemed irremediable, she
cleaned Humbert's room with a particular thoroughness, as
some peasant woman might polish the last remaining shrine
of the old faith in a sea of vandalism.

'Mrs Goodenough,' said Miriam, 'why do you waste
so much time on Mr Stukeley's room? He's not coming
back for ages.'

'Because,' said Mrs Goodenough, 'Mr Stukeley likes his
things kept nice.' She spoke as if this were some *ex cathedra*
pronouncement by he-who-must-be-obeyed. Indeed, Miriam
remembered that, on her only meeting with Humbert, he
had said: 'I'm not fussy, but I do like a certain amount
of order in my environment.' This was untrue. He was
fussy.

'But don't you find all this housework a frightful drag?'
said Miriam, leaning on the doorpost, chewing an apple
and scratching herself meditatively.

'A servant with this clause makes drudgery divine.
That's what they taught me in school,' said Mrs Goodenough, glaring at Miriam's nightdress whose frilled hem
bounced saucily around her thighs. 'And now if you'll
excuse me, Miss Stettin, *I've* got work to do.' She started
operations with the vacuum cleaner whose powerful whine
prevented further conversation. Miriam reminded herself
to tell George how marvellously Mrs Goodenough's

stiff-corseted behind could express disapproval. Was it natural, or the result of conscious muscular control? Mrs Goodenough was certainly not life-enhancing.

Miriam's relationship with George had now reached a satisfactory stage. In bed, they had advanced from the formalities of congress with its protocols and differences of opinion over the agenda. The language barrier which so often impedes international meetings had been overcome. They had progressed through the smooth exchanges which characterize intercourse between acquaintances who find each other sympathetic and want to know one another better. They were now definitely intimate. Their attainment of pleasure was nearly simultaneous. But there were still surprises in their lovemaking. Chance changes of position and emphasis still produced unexpected delights.

And then there was the mystery of Miriam's womanhood. His previous sexual encounters had mostly been with reckless but reticent Winkhill girls whose lust was mainly for experience. They had not confided their womanly problems in him. Their boisterousness was as yet unstained by the bitterness of the sex war. Their golden limbs did not ache with the burdens of love and marriage.

But Miriam was very interested in being a woman. In fact, it was one of her main interests. She managed to communicate her enthusiasm to George so that many of their evenings together were spent discussing such questions as: do all married women tend to vegetate? If so, should they? Can a woman be both independent and happy? Are women more dishonest than men? Are they more religious? Is it only lack of opportunity that has prevented women from achieving success in art? Can a man ever love as deeply as a woman, e.g. the Portuguese nun? Do men like women? Do women like men?

These discussions George found dangerous as well as intellectually stimulating. The conversation changed so quickly from the general to the particular (further question : why do women always take everything personally?).

'I think,' said George, 'that women are all so preoccupied with the problems of sex or the family or whatever you like to call the whole thing that they haven't got time to think of intellectual activity as anything more than a diversion. Lots of girls just memorize the names of the Impressionists in order to attract the egghead beaux. In the same way, other girls learn to play tennis so as to meet athletic bank-clerks at the local tennis club. They're merely aiming at different markets.'

'I see,' said Miriam, 'you think the only reason I learn anything is so as to be able to hop into bed with as many different sorts of men as possible. I'm just a plaything to you. You don't seem to realize that sort of line went out with Queen Victoria.'

'Certain things don't change,' said George airily.

'You among them. You're insufferably complacent.'

'At least I'm able to discuss things rationally without inventing imaginary insults and losing my temper.'

'I was merely pursuing the logical implications of your remarks. I can't help it if you don't know what you're talking about.'

Such playful dialogues had become a stimulating feature of their relationship. Did they, George wondered as he sat in the Tube, contain the seeds of serious conflict? The girl sitting opposite hadn't really got such bad legs at all. Her mouth had a nice mischievous look about it. And her hair was lovely. No, he must shake these disloyal thoughts out of his mind and before he got to Mansion

House too, otherwise they would be with him for the rest of the day.

George walked up Leadenhall Street to his office. Around him City men were scurrying to work with nervous steps as if the streets were paved not with gold but with some substance that might stick to their shoes if too heavily trodden. In the office which he shared with George, Evan Pratt was reading the *Financial Times*.

He looked up.

' You've chosen a bad morning to be late, boy. Timmy's been asking for you for twenty minutes.'

' Oh. Any idea why?'

' He looked so kind and understanding that I thought he must be giving you the sack. But that's looking on the bright side, mind. You never know what these capitalists are up to,' said Evan. The conspiracy theory of life was one of the main props of his cheerfulness.

George walked slowly along the deep-carpeted passage leading to the partners' rooms. He slowed down his breathing and smoothed his hair. Nothing was worse than to arrive panting and dishevelled. He put on his young executive's face – energy and intelligence spiced with a dash of low cunning.

Timmy Le Mercier was leaning back in his armchair looking blankly at the large Jackson Pollock which the bank had just bought in order to show its interest in the arts. Though it was only ten a.m., he was demonstrating his rude vitality by smoking a fat cigar. Seen through the smoke, his pale round face resembled the moon veiled by cloud.

' Good morning, George. Come in and take a pew. Good of you to look in on me. I thought it was about time we had a chat. As you know, I've been out of the office quite a lot recently what with one thing and another. These things mount up. One gets snowed under by the bumf and bored stiff by the argy-bargy. And you don't get a minute to yourself.'

He seemed temporarily to lose interest in what he was saying. He tapped his cigar on the edge of a silver ash-tray in the shape of a baseball glove. His unseeing eyes returned to the Jackson Pollock. He was casting about for a new line of attack. George said nothing but looked even more energetic and intelligent. Timmy Le Mercier leant forward, confidingly, man-to-man.

' Quite frankly, George, I get the impression that you're not too happy with us at the moment. Of course we're very glad that you came here. But I do like to feel that the Bank is a happy ship, if that's not too corny a way of putting it. And dissatisfaction among the crew does, I'm afraid, spread, and spread very quickly sometimes.'

' I'm not starting a mutiny on the quarterdeck, I can promise you that,' said George, jocularly.

' No, I didn't mean that, old boy. But, if I may say so, you haven't been doing terribly well in the last few weeks. No Gestapo stuff of course, ha ha, but you have been late fifteen times, on one occasion, more than an hour-and-a-half late – '

' Dentist,' said George.

' Two files mislaid, figures wrong on the Dresden-Jebb deal and Mrs Watkinson has twice complained to the Chief Clerk of your discourtesy. And if I may end on a rather personal note, old boy, your hair is just a bit long. This isn't the army of course, but we do rely on creating confidence to get more business. And I'm afraid that in this wicked world personal appearance does count in these matters. Superficial, perhaps, but that's the way it is.'

George said he would get his hair cut and try to be more punctual.

'Good, good. But these are just details, symptoms if you like. The real question is: do you feel you have a future with us here in the Bank? If you do, no one would be more pleased than myself. We shall make the best use we can of your talents. On the other hand, if you think your talents could be better employed elsewhere, we can make alternative arrangements. The choice is entirely yours.' Le Mercier indicated with an extended hand the infinite range of possibilities open to George.

George said he would think it over.

'Was it the sack?' asked Evan Pratt sympathetically on George's return.

'In essence but not in form. I can stay on here if I'm prepared to swab out the partners' latrines.'

'Ah, yes, we shall make the best use we can of your talents. I remember he tried that one on me once, when we'd had a bit of a dust-up. I told him if he wanted to keep a first-class Welsh economist, he would have to treat him as a first-class Welsh economist, and not put him on the bloody filing-cabinets. We had no more trouble after that.' Evan's eyes shone at the memory of his heroic class-encounter.

'Well, I think I'm going to push off. I can't stand Timmy and I can't stand banking.'

'That's right, boy. Get out while there's time. You desert the sinking ship of capitalism before she finally goes down. You're all right with your fat private income. You've got economic freedom. But I'm just a poor lad from the valleys who's got to make his way in the world.'

George decided to ring up Major McCambridge. After a few exchanges with secretaries and personal assistants, Mc-

Cambridge's voice came down the line, strong and entre-
preneurial.

George wondered whether McCambridge remembered
their conversation about Skreenjingles. He had been
thinking it over. If there was still a possibility of employment in that line, he would be very interested.

'Indeed I remember it very well, very well,' said Major
McCambridge, stalling. 'I'm very glad you rang me up.
Of course, I can't promise anything. The situation may
have changed since I've been away. These growing
companies seesaw about so much, you know. But I'll sniff
around a bit and let you know how things stand when
you come back from your Biarritz trip. What about that?'

George said he was very grateful and rang off. Not a
promising start at all. It was perhaps not surprising that
McCambridge should know his plans. At the same time
it was irritating. McCambridge's power seemed to be ex-
tending into the recesses of George's private life as well as
controlling his hopes of employment.

The Biarritz trip had only just been arranged. Professor
Stettin was wont to protect his delicate chest from autumnal
fog by a few weeks in the sun. He stayed with a distant
cousin and admirer, Solange Lévy, the widow of a French
textile magnate. Besides her large villa in the hills, Mme
Lévy had a cottage down in Arrèche which was equipped
for writers who wished to write. The writers had not turned
up in their expected numbers, so the cottage was being lent
to Miriam and Ray. George Whale and Annabel Meyer
as current stable companions were also invited. George saw
the whole expedition as an untrammelled idyll. At the least,
it would be better than the ski-ing holiday with conventional, unloved acquaintances which he had previously
projected. McCambridge's knowledge of his plans wiped

the bloom off the idyll. His wishes for George's enjoyment had contained a hint of lecherous envy. Within the limits of the telephone, Major McCambridge had winked.

Le Mercier came into the office to collect George for the monthly meeting of a company to whom the bank acted as advisers. Normally it was Evan's job to act as Le Mercier's lieutenant on these occasions. But he was occupied with more important things. George got out the papers and followed Le Mercier.

Timmy Le Mercier never took the lift. He pretended that the daily ascent and descent of three flights of stairs was his only opportunity for taking exercise, so tight was his schedule. In fact he had a secret work-out in a Soho gymnasium every Thursday. He was rather drawn to the rough company.

As he bounded down the stairs, his round face was caught by the wall-lights on each landing so that he appeared to twinkle like a silver coin spinning along a pavement. They were swept through the revolving doors and into the waiting car. The chauffeur smoothed the rug over Le Mercier's knees as if packing a valuable work of art.

As they jerked and crawled westward towards the Euston Road, Le Mercier looked out of the window at the passing scene with a flickering intensity.

' That woman has chosen the wrong hat. She's the sort of woman who always chooses the wrong hat . . . another Chinese restaurant. Extraordinary success they're having. Keep their costs very low, that's the secret . . . four road signs on the same corner, each costing £10 or £20 and taking a couple of men half a day to install. Why not have more multiple signs on the same base – Keep left, No parking, traffic lights – all on the same stalk.'

The idea caught his own fancy. He switched on the

dictaphone and repeated his words in a more urgent, coherent form into the gleaming microphone. He took up the rambling commentary again.

' Pulling the old Midland building down already. Who's developing that, I wonder? The office space should be fairly cheap. Close to the West End. All this part of London is due for upgrading. Fact, George. But how do we use that fact?'

He turned to George, looking not so much for an answer as for signs of admiration of his questing, Faustian mind. George suggested that the quarter could be torn down and replaced by a pedestrian shopping precinct with office and residential space above it.

' No money in it, George. Not a bean. People don't like quiet, restful places to shop. They want excitement, speed, noise, flickering colours. They want to be dazzled, tempted. If you could run a motorway right through your super-market, turnover would double immediately.'

They drew up at a faceless office block in the Euston Road. In his own office Timmy Le Mercier's manner was comradely, even jovial. On foreign territory he was different. He waited stiffly while the commissionaire held open the door, and he inclined his head with a dignified half-smile to the pretty girl who shepherded them to the boardroom. He did not comment to George by word or gesture on the way her bottom wiggled. He behaved like a British Monarch on a state visit to some newly independent nation whose pride must not be wounded by suggestions of Imperialist mockery.

George and Timmy were sat at one end of the table, with the directors on the other three sides. They were hemmed in by a blank wall of solid faces. Indeed, as they sat down, Timmy Le Mercier's own round face took on the same bricklike impassivity. Only George's untidy hair marred the symmetry of smoothness.

The chairman had a long, thin face and that shifty air which the strain of honest broking can impose on middle-aged industrialists.

Minutes were read. Some query about the agenda was raised. The chairman settled it mournfully. A new director was to be welcomed to the board. It was Major McCambridge. His entry subtly combined briskness and diffidence.

Everyone shook hands.

' Didn't expect to see you here, George.'

' I didn't expect to see you either.'

' Why on earth not?' said Major McCambridge impatiently, as if someone had expressed surprise at seeing Nelson's Column in Trafalgar Square.

' Well, gentlemen, let us proceed to the main business of the meeting,' said the chairman, who already seemed weary of the strains of office. ' The question – or shall I say the possibility – of the company acquiring a stake of an extent to be decided in Rubber Borings Limited. We have of course conducted our own enquiries into RB and its problems. But perhaps Grainger Le Mercier would like to give us their views to set the ball rolling. Timmy.'

Le Mercier launched himself. It was fluent, accurate, well-documented – and yet somehow totally unreal, the picture that he presented of Rubber Borings. George himself had only flipped through the figures, as it was Evan Pratt who had done the main research. Yet he had got a clear impression that Rubber Borings was an albatross, easy to bag but impossible to get rid of, once acquired. Merely to keep it going would require a lot of money. To make it a sound, competitive outfit might cost as much as to start an identical firm from scratch. Yet for some reason Le Mercier was keen that these solid men at this solid table should squander shareholders' money on this apparently doom-laden enterprise. Why?

The bank was acting only as industrial adviser. They might also take on the financing of the deal if it was agreed to. But Le Mercier had not made a substantial reputation for shrewdness by touting for business in this way. Could the reason be that Rubber Borings was better than it looked?

The solid men conferred, they doodled, they leant across to each other, temporizing with questions:

'What is our cash position likely to be at the end of the account?'

'Could we close down the small works?'

' – or perhaps diversity and then – '

'Dispose of the outstanding sub-contracting work – '

'Can we be certain that *all* their board would chuck their hands in?'

They did everything but come to a decision. The solid men melted into one gluey mass as soon as there was any chance of individual responsibility – and later blame – being assigned. They gloried in the collective principle.

McCambridge had been playing – almost overplaying – the part of the new boy on the board. He murmured 'Jolly good point' whenever the Chairman spoke. When the senior member of the Board, a wizened man with an erroneous moustache, rang for coffee, he leant across to McCambridge and said:

'We generally have a cup of coffee at about this time.'

And McCambridge said: 'What a splendid idea' – and rubbed his hands together, enchanted by the ingenuity of this arrangement.

'That is, unless you'd prefer tea.'

'No, no, coffee would be splendid.'

Yet through this fog of bonhomie, it gradually became apparent that McCambridge was not in agreement with Le Mercier.

Little things at first. 'I wonder if you'd mind giving us those figures again, Timmy.' Then – 'when you say the company's turnover was steady, do you mean steady or stagnant?' Until finally the definitive McCambridge position was unveiled, well hedged around with qualifications.

'I must confess that with all due respect to my new colleagues who obviously know a great deal more about this matter than me, I do not entirely at this moment – and I emphasize at this moment – grasp the exact reason why we should be contemplating the purchase of a stake, even a minority holding, in a company which is losing money. If we can get it cheap and make it pay, very well and good. But so far nobody seems very convinced that we can make it pay. Would it not be rather like (pausing for a striking comparison) throwing good money after bad? In my humble submission, I would have thought there was at least a case for delaying the decision until we have a look at their figures for the half-year. After all, there's time enough. Rubber Borings won't bounce away from our grasp, ha, ha.'

A flutter of relief ran through the solid men. The chairman looked shiftier than ever – he moved his head from side to side apprehensively, as if speculating which of two rival detachments of the Fraud Squad would catch up with him first. He himself had first floated the idea of buying a stake in Rubber Borings. As a child, he had had a Mickey Mouse bicycle tyre repair kit made by RB.

The solid men genially agreed to McCambridge's suggestion. Delay and indecision were their natural elements, and McCambridge had made a good impression by showing himself to be at home in those elements.

The meeting moved on to the other topic affecting Grainger Le Mercier. Should the company broaden its retail outlets in West Africa? Without such outlets, their prospects of expanding their export market in that region were small. And yet recent changes in the system of double taxation relief meant that such an investment would not be profitable. They would have to pay tax – admittedly at a reduced rate – in Britain as well as in Africa. Opinion was divided. The chairman in particular seemed doubtful. He gave the impression that whatever they did, it was unlikely to be legal, that if they were not arrested and jailed in Britain, some worse fate would await them in Lagos.

Le Mercier blandly displayed facts and figures whenever the discussion lagged. Though as an adviser his role might seem subservient to that of the decision-makers, his graciousness was such that he had the air of a variety star willing to delight his public with an infinity of encores.

Then McCambridge struck.

' I must confess,' he said, looking down demurely into his clasped hands resting strongly on the mahogany, ' that I cannot understand this government. It is supposed to be friendly to the interests of us business people. They claim to be grateful for the contribution we make to the prosperity of this country, both in tangible exports and in invisible earnings. And yet their every move seems designed to throttle our export markets and to lose that international confidence which makes Britain the changing-house of the world. I can only describe these changes in the system of double tax relief as iniquitous and half-baked.' Rising to a baritone crescendo – 'what the hell's the point of us working our arses off when every penny we earn goes to build palatial council houses for snivelling layabouts? I don't wish to exaggerate, but I can only call it a crying scandal.'

He leant back in his chair, slightly red in the face. The effect was superb. Murmurs of agreement from the solid men. The sales director with occupational over-enthusiasm, smacked the table with the palm of his hand. McCambridge's wrath had been beautifully modulated – fierce enough to indicate his reserves of character, not too violent to embarrass his audience. It was this suggestion of control which contrasted so strongly with the flatulent indignation of Professor Stettin and the peevish irritation of Hervey or Cynthia Whale.

The solid men were now in McCambridge's pocket. In one board meeting, he had managed to show himself as a man of judgement not afraid to speak his mind – with that useful glint of the rough diamond beneath.

As the meeting broke up, McCambridge said to George :

' We must have a talk about that job some time, George. Rather busy at the moment, but I won't let it out of my mind, never you fear.'

He smiled. He had time for everyone.

George and Le Mercier drove back to the office.

' Why did you load the scales in favour of the RB deal?' asked George.

' Because I think it's a good thing. I have a notion they could be on the verge of a slight upswing. And with decent management it could make money, though I admit the figures don't look much that way yet. Also, our clients have got more money than they know what to do with, and, yellow-bellied though they are, they will have to buy something with it. As they are also mean as hell, they will want to buy it cheap. And RB's about the only cheap proposition in their line of country at the moment. So I think they will buy RB. In which case, we want to make it clear that it was Grainger's who advised them to do so. Even if our advice turns out to be wrong – which is an even money chance – that is better than being disregarded. Once those sort of people have dared to go against their advisers, they may also dare to get rid of them. And we don't want that, do we?'

'But with McCambridge against the idea, will they get it through?'

'I think you'll find that, in a month or two,' said Le Mercier, 'Jack will emerge as the main proponent of the scheme. I should imagine he wanted to hold them off a decision today until he's got a proper grip on them. It doesn't do to have your colleagues deciding things while you merely tag along.'

'Just suppose you and McCambridge are wrong about RB, won't they make you carry the can?'

'Of course. But they will be pleased to have shuffled off the responsibility. And, once shuffled off, responsibility is hard to regain. Decisions, right or wrong, are after all decisions.'

George sank back into his seat, brooding over the mysteries of commerce.

'Jack McCambridge,' said Le Mercier, 'is an odd man. Very successful, of course. He might over-extend himself one day, though I doubt it. Some personal upset – his wife running off with his chauffeur, something like that – could crack him. But then that can crack anyone. Jarvis, could you drive a little faster.

'McCambridge is a real entrepreneur, you know, one of

the boys who really take the risks. Not like you or me, George,' patting George's arm, ' we can go where the money is. We can use it when we get there. But we don't create it. In a sense, our sort is better fitted to public service – politics, the armed services, that kind of thing. There is something rather apologetic about our attempts to make a little money. Somehow one's education seemed to be based on the belief that one already has enough – which one certainly didn't after one's father's business went bust.

' Still, I suppose I've been born to the life, straight from the war into the City. Never a question of anything else. My father was in it too before the crash, a bullion broker. But not like McCambridge, either of us. None of that rest-lessness, what is vulgarly known as drive. I imagine it must be to do with his lower middle class background – genteel poverty, you know, the struggle to keep up. Well, it's certainly got him somewhere, while we merely lubricate the wheels of industry, and hope that our palm gets a little greased in the process.'

He scratched an eyebrow and looked out of the window, his blank eyes tracking a tall girl swaying along Cheap-side.

As the car drew up at the bank, Le Mercier turned to George and said sharply :

' You will of course treat our conversation as entirely confidential. Jack McCambridge is an old friend of mine, as well as a business colleague. And you will also, I hope, remember what I said to you earlier this morning. Flashes of inspiration are no substitute for hard work.'

George appeared to be thrust out into the cold again.

He spent the afternoon comparing the performance over the last decade of H. J. Thwaite & Co with that of other manufacturers of cleansing agents. He then compared their probable performance, capital requirements and expansion potential for the next ten years. Timmy Le Mercier had indeed said that their American clients were very happy with George's previous work on Thwaite's but they had felt that he had not quite depicted the big picture. How, they had enquired, was the detergent situation industry-wise? George set out to answer this question. It was uphill work. The balance sheets of their great companies with their subsidiary acolytes were oracular. As an art form, double-entry book-keeping was superb; the antiphonal formulae – paid-up capital, cash in hand and at bank, net depreciation at factor cost and dividend after tax – culminated so finely in that dialectical synthesis at the bottom of the page where assets and liabilities agreed in one huge improbable figure. But the essential questions, whether the company was doing well, whether it was efficiently run, these were not answered. Though the truth was doubtless in there somewhere, it was not lightly revealed to profane eyes.

At a quarter to four, tea came round.

'Not the cracked cup again, Vivienne.'

'This isn't the Ritz, Mr Whale.'

Soon after tea, George abandoned the detergents and took out a file marked Personal from the bottom drawer of his desk. The Personal File contained two newspaper pictures of Marilyn Monroe already yellowing with age and sentiment, letters from girls who had written to him – only one hurried note from Miriam so far – and George's poems. These works, few in number and uneven in quality, were united only by the fact that they had all been written in office hours. They included a savage Swiftian attack on Timmy Le Mercier, a sonnet on *Petite Étoile*, the filly of the century, and a rollicking ballad on the Ministry of Economic Co-operation. There were several love poems written to Sally Meredith whom he had once kissed and who was now married to a socially conscious playwright. He was a successful playwright which had made it worse at the time.

The latest poem had been finished yesterday and was cooler in tone. It was called The Private Eye Reflects:

Idling my way thru an evening shower
circling on myself beneath the spray
I unwound my thoughts and wondered
how best to separate my body
from the shadow of the nude Verena
dead fallen across the dressing-table
in the Park Avenue apartment.

The unemphatic muscle now stood clear
and the showermists closed over
the tanned breasts the golden hair
and the greenbacks fluttering from the suitcase
I moved from behind the shower-curtain
to a towel and bourbon on the rocks.

George wondered whether there might not be some parallel traceable between the modern hero-narcissus figure of the private detective and Roland, his eighth-century counterpart. Would the poem be improved by some reference to the legend? To insert, ' *Dieu, que le son du cor est triste, le soir, au fond des bois* ' might be a bit too literary. On the whole, the poem was better left to stand by itself.

On reviewing his oeuvre, George was struck by the undoubted talent shown. It would be a pity to let it run to waste. Journalism could be the answer. Ray might perhaps be able to find him an outlet. True, Ray was only working on the managerial side of the newspaper business. On the other hand, he was making so much money that he must have attained a certain amount of influence by now.

A quarter past five. Almost time to go. Without that indecent haste which created such a bad impression in office life, George started packing up. He carefully locked away the Personal File and replaced the balance sheets in their folders. As he went along the passage to wash, he passed Timmy Le Mercier and Strachey, the Chief Clerk, who was looking harassed and old.

' But Mr Timothy, if we don't finish the accounts today, the books will have closed by – '

' Don't worry, Strachey,' Le Mercier put an affectionate arm round Strachey's bent shoulders, ' we'll all end up in the workhouse together.'

George wondered whether there was a workhouse in Roquebrune where Timmy Le Mercier had his summer shack.

Back in the flat, Miriam was sitting on the floor by the electric fire, taking exaggeratedly long drags at a cigarette. The tide of books scattered around the room had risen since the morning. Miriam's method of broadening her horizons was to read half-a-dozen pages of each of the world's Thousand Best Books. These eclectic sniffs at the elixir of literature would in due course surround her with an over-whelming perfume of cultivation. Her day's reading had included the Critique of Pure Reason, the Cod of the Woosters, L'Être et le Néant, Afternoon Men and the Golden Bough.

She jumped up catlike when George came in and put her arms round his neck. They adopted with pleasure their roles in the child's game of happy families. George, while enjoying his part as the bread-winner, noted that Miriam had hardly embraced the maxim that a woman's work is never done. The apple-core motif was enriched by a series of half-empty coffee cups which set a delicate obstacle course around the room.

'Naice day at the office, dear?' asked Miriam.

'Not bad, dear. I got the sack, that's all,' said George, burying his face in his hands.

'The sack, dear? Oh, my poor Georgy-Porgy,' said Miriam, continuing the novelette dialogue with relish.

'Seriously, yes, in a way. Timmy Le Mercier said in his subtle fashion that I could stay on if I pulled up my socks to what would obviously be an unendurable extent. So I thought the time had come to move on.'

'How awful. So what are you going to do?'

'Well, I talked to Jack McCambridge to see if he had anything to offer. Through the cloud of suavity, I managed to gather that he hadn't.'

'How odd. Ray rang up today and said that a ridiculous man called McCambridge had offered him a job running something called Skreenjingles.'

'Oh.'

'Ray said it sounded a pretty good con. But the pay was so fabulous he couldn't turn it down.'

'Oh.'

'He also said he's got a postcard from Dada. Apparently it's raining in Arrèche and Solange is drunk most of the time. She's also got a new man, a dazzling Italian called Alvise Dall'Umbria. He's an electric prince.'

'What do you mean?'

'He's a prince and his father makes light bulbs.'

Already George had a vivid picture of Arrèche. A dark, precipice-encurled village, beaten by a perpetual thunderstorm intermittently lit by flashes of lightning from celestial light-bulbs. Across the screen reeled Mme Lévy, drunk and preceded by an enormous Jewish nose, while Professor Stettin limped behind, his ascetic features contorted in his passion for Mme Lévy. Above them, lolling in a chariot strung with giant fairy lights, the Electric Prince shouted insults at his minions. *Walpurgisnacht* as depicted by Cecil B. de Mille.

Still, it would be better than going ski-ing with Humbert Stukeley and his stolid sister.

Chapter 6

The morning jet from Hamburg to Berlin flew over the North German plain. In a first class seat with a gin and tonic at his elbow sat Hervey Whale. He was doing his constituency correspondence. This weekly event was arduous but satisfying. The complaints and congratulations which rolled in from constituents from all walks of life gave him a feeling of contact. Through these ill-spelt spidery manuscripts he reached out to that heterogeneous mass whose only common feature was that by a majority vote three years earlier they had returned H. J. Whale (Conservative) to Parliament.

At his side sat his personal secretary, Miss Curvis, her pen hovering over her shorthand pad and her tweed skirt frowning over her knees. The first letter was rather carelessly typed. It read:

17 Lanyon Terrace, S.W.3

' Honoured sir,

As a graduate (1948) of the Birmingham School of Metallurgical Engineering, I send you Almighty Blessings and all good Happiness. I do not wish to invade your privacy, but there are matters beyond my control which demand your attention.

My egregious landlord, Mr Karopoulos, wishes to evict me out of my residence on the grounds of noise and nocturnal disturbance. But I entertain only my sister from Stockwell and her husband, a highly respectable man. We sometimes play a little Bach and talk of good books. But Karopoulos says he knows ways and means to evict me. What ways please? He also wishes to double my rent which is already grossly excessive.

I hear of rent tribunals but cannot find the tribunal-house. I turn to you for help.

Yours despairing servant
Rabindanath Chatri.'

In a measured, friendly, reply Hervey referred Mr. Chatri to the Embankment Citizens' Advice Bureau who would most certainly put him in touch with the local rent tribunal and advise him on his legal position. He returned Mr Chatri's good wishes.

The next letter was from a Mrs Macdonald. It was about the rising cost of living: 'coal up, fares up, groceries up, rent up, I don't know how you expect me to keep a decent home on £11 a week my husband is a bus-driver. The biggest mistake we ever made was to put you lot into Parliament.' In his answer Hervey thanked her for her letter and said that prices looked like steadying down a bit.

The third letter was written in a shaky hand on lined paper. The letter was spaced as if in some free verse form. There was a good deal of underlining.

' I am a man *past the 70 years of age*
I have in recent years *suffered a major*

operation taking part of *internal away*
I have been and experienced a knock down
on Road by Car and *picked up from*
paralysed position with the car wheels
moving to a stop a few inches from my
chest for this I received a *few pills*
in a box prescription after X rays
I try to *carry on for the best* with my
remaining bit of life it being the only
INCOME I have *signed on*
So WHY should a *deprivation time*
cruelty worry be *meted out to me*
to the *last point* and *the money* not
in my hands thats for *shelter from*
cold exposure at night they know where its gone
Should these people that have signed
on the bigger INCOME *possess a key*
for *my comfort* let them by all means
step forward *and place the key in my hands.*'

It was certainly puzzling. The references to signing on
implied some misunderstanding with the National Assistance Board. The key motif suggested more landlord
difficulty. Perhaps a combination of the two. Yet if the
NAB's officers had investigated the case, as they would
have, there was really no more that Hervey could do. On
the other hand, merely to admit his impotence and express
his regret was too off-hand, too callous. The writer was
clearly in genuine distress.

Hervey noticed with relief that the letter had no address
at the top and was unsigned. He could do no more.

The remaining letters were from retired government
servants complaining about the inadequacies of their

pensions. There were also three or four from female supporters telling him how much they had enjoyed his address at the Annual General Meeting. Hervey dictated his replies quickly, then dismissed Miss Curvis and started looking out of the window.

Below there was nothing to see except lines of conifers straggling across an endless sandy waste. They looked rather like the hair of his personal assistant, Cruddace-Smith, who was sitting behind him reading the *Guardian* of the previous day.

Hervey Whale's European tour had so far passed without incident. In Brussels he had sat in on a session of the Agricultural Exchange Commission. They were discussing potato prices and the session had ended in amicable deadlock. In Hamburg he had attended the opening of a new dock intended principally for British oil tankers. And now he was flying to Berlin for the Tariff Equalization Conference. Hervey was enjoying himself. He moved as on a conveyor belt from aeroplane to official reception to press conference to private high-level discussions to cocktails to official dinner to hotel to bed. He was briefed on the people he was to meet, on the line he ought to take and the manner in which he ought to take it. Nothing was left to chance or personal failing. Hervey became temporarily a personage, a star. It was most relaxing.

The aeroplane began to descend. Berlin with its generous girdle of woods came into sight. Hervey got up. Cruddace-Smith handed him his overcoat.

'James,' said Hervey as he put it on, 'who's going to meet us at the airport?'

'Only Bonhoeffer, Minister, and the British Minister in Berlin, of course.'

'What do we know of Bonhoeffer, James?'

Cruddace-Smith adjusted his square horn-rimmed spectacles – a nervous gesture which always preceded any personal judgement.

'The F.O. think him rather unreliable, Minister. We were rather surprised when he got the Economic Co-operation job in the last Bonn shake-up.' And the same, reflected, Cruddace-Smith, might be said of the Whale. Cruddace-Smith and his wife Monica sustained a fantasy saga about Hervey in which he was referred to as Moby Dick or, on the postcards he sent to Monica during idle moments in the Ministry, as M.D. The Prime Minister was Captain Ahab. Cruddace-Smith himself was Ishmael. After making love in their Islington flat, the Cruddace-Smiths would elaborate indelicate stories of the Great White Whale thrashing about in sexual waters.

'Unreliable?' asked Hervey, probingly.

'Misuse of development funds, I believe, Minister. They also say he's drinking too much and in public.'

'Ah, I see,' said Hervey, 'just the occupational hazards of public life.' He sat down in his seat again and fastened his safety belt.

The aeroplane landed and, after some apparently random taxi-ing along the runways, stopped outside the terminal.

Herr Bonhoeffer, a burly man in a check overcoat, burst through the glass doors of the waiting lounge like an impatient wasp. The head of the British mission followed at a diplomatic pace.

Until one had shaken hands with genial Herr Bonhoeffer, thought Hervey, one did not know what real insincerity was. Hervey and Cruddace-Smith felt their shields of British reticence being blown away by the gale of his cordiality.

'A good trip, Herr Minister? You look in the pink. But you British are so resilient. And Mr Smith – a real pleasure.'

'Cruddace-Smith,' said Cruddace-Smith, clicking his heels together.

'We hope to give you a good time in Berlin. The Conference promises well – magnificently well. So many representatives of our underdeveloped friends.' With a wave of his hand, Herr Bonhoeffer indicated imaginary legions of the hungry thronging the empty airfield.

Inside the lounge, Herr Bonhoeffer looked a good deal less dynamic. His silvery hair which had blown so gallantly in the wind outside was thinning. The shoulders of his smart suit were speckled with scurf. And his strong florid face was networked with broken veins.

Gradually the conveyor belt of public life gathered momentum – the government Mercedes drove them to the hotel, where Cruddace-Smith barely had time to drop his daily postcard to Monica. 'At eight bells today the Great White Whale encountered the fearsome Bonhoeffer shark. The Almighty alone can know the outcome, Yr Ishmael.'

In the hall of the hotel, Hervey saw a man in a camel-hair coat sitting at a coffee-table talking urgently to two impassive Slavs. It was McCambridge.

'Hullo Jack,' said Hervey, taking the offensive. 'What brings you to this divided city?'

'Why, Good Lord, it's Hervey. Here for the tariff beano, I suppose. I'm just mending a few of the fences you politicians sit on. Cementing East-West relations with cement-mixers, old boy. You must meet my partners in crime, Mr Plekhov, Mr Zabresti – Mr Whale, Her Majesty's Minister for Economic Co-operation.'

They shook hands. Mr Zabresti said it was a great pleasure. Mr Plekhov said it was a great honour. Hervey bowed.

'Well, I'm afraid I can't stop and chat, Jack. I've got

107

an official lunch to get through. Could we meet later?'

' Sorry, old boy. Off to Moscow in half-an-hour. Watch the gastric juices and give my love to Cynthia.'

' I will. Good-bye for now.'

Hervey went into the private dining-table with the inner glow of world citizenship. It was nice to meet old friends in odd parts of the world. Though of course Jack Mc-Cambridge could hardly be considered as an old friend. Cynthia had produced him only six months or so ago. He seemed a bit shifty on first meeting but his bonhomie wore one down in the end. He was a good businessman anyway, that might be useful when one got tired of politics. Besides, Cynthia was usually a sound judge of character and it was a tribute to old Jack that she should have bothered to ask him to dinner and even suggest that he might like a day's shooting at Gravell. She did not normally initiate social activity.

The lunch was almost as heavy as the session of the Conference that followed. Hervey tried to explain the liquidity problem in French to the Moroccan delegate. The Moroccan delegate thought he was making unfounded allegations about the oil resources of the Sahara. It was most exhausting.

Then something was wrong with the earphones in the Conference Hall. The translation of Herr Bonhoeffer's speech of welcome was interrupted by an involved conversation between two of the interpreters about the lateness of the coffee break. Hervey switched off the earphones. At his side, Cruddace-Smith was tapping his teeth with the end of his pen. Hervey glared at him. Cruddace-Smith, expecting some whispered instruction, leant across. Hervey fended him off with an enigmatic smile. Cruddace-Smith started tapping again.

Eventually Hervey was called upon to read out his speech with its Nine-Point Plan for World Trade. It was quite a good plan. With luck, Hervey thought, it might be remembered as the Whale Plan. Unfortunately, it was not remembered at all. The thunder was stolen by the Italian plan which only had Three Points, all easily memorized and virtually meaningless. The Whale plan was too concrete; it aroused opposition on all sides. The civil servants who had concocted the Whale Plan blamed Hervey for his lacklustre presentation of the plan. Hervey blamed the civil servants for their lack of political acumen.

When they returned to the hotel, Herr Bonhoeffer was already standing at the bar with a large whisky in his hand. His face had become somewhat redder.

' Ah, good evening, my friends. Come and join me in a little cocktail.' He waved the dark-brown glass of whisky. Glasses were brought for Hervey and Cruddace-Smith.

' An exhausting session, Herr Whale. But constructive. What did you think of my speech ?'

' Both interesting and eloquent.'

' Really, you thought so? Your plan, if I may say so, was most constructive and delivered with that *typisch* British dignity.'

Herr Bonhoeffer handed round some small but powerful Dutch cigars, saying : ' I think you will like these special Willems. A most constructive cigar.'

The party or, to be more accurate, Herr Bonhoeffer, was warming up. He forecast ' an evening of intimate pleasure ' for himself and Herr Whale. As a necessary prelude to this, Cruddace-Smith withdrew from the party and went to an Italian film on the Kurfürstendamm. It was about proletarian life in industrial Lombardy. The sound-track broke down, but the passions of the protagonists were on the whole expressed visually. It had the combination of sauciness and social realism which appealed to Cruddace-Smith. Afterwards, he wrote another postcard to Monica : ' Moby Dick has slipped his harpoon and is now basking in tropical waters in the wake of the Bonhoeffer shark.'

Herr Bonhoeffer had another tumbler of whisky. He invited Hervey to call him ' Dietrich '. In return for this pleasure, he begged to be allowed to address Herr Whale as ' Hervé '.

They moved on to a little Alsatian restaurant called ' Chez Tillich '. Herr Bonhoeffer explained why his first marriage had gone wrong. His wife had come from Bremen, a dull foggy port. She had not appreciated Herr Bonhoeffer's Bavarian lightness and gaiety. She had cooked and knitted while he, then a penniless law student, had been the toast of the Munich intelligentsia. She had disappeared during the unpleasantness of the Thirties. He had not seen her since. Herr Bonhoeffer wiped away a tear.

A sad-eyed guitarist was now wandering through the tables. Herr Bonhoeffer clasped his hands.

' Do you know some Italian songs ?'

' Si, Signor.'

' I wonder if you know the one I mean. It was a great favourite of my late wife. Santa Luigi.'

' Santa Lucia ?'

' No. No. Santa Luigi. It is a famous song. It goes like this – Sa-anta Lui-i-igi.' Herr Bonhoeffer's baritone was strong. The cutlery rattled.

' Yes, I know it, signor.'

The guitarist sang Santa Lucia, his thin voice slurring over syllables of the chorus. When he had finished, Herr Bonhoeffer clapped very loudly and shouted to the guitarist. ' Ecco, Santa Luigi !'

The guitarist smiled sadly.

As they walked down the street to the *Kabarett* where they were to have a nightcap, Herr Bonhoeffer explained why his second marriage was going wrong.

'She is a neurotic bitch, you know. Not constructive at all. Is it surprising that I should take my pleasure elsewhere? A public man has a duty to relax and so keep fit.'

Hervey did not feel fit. The sudden cold of the night made him feel weak at the knees. The second bottle of burgundy had been a mistake. And the brandy on top of that a disaster. Would Herr Bonhoeffer think him insufficiently resilient if he just had soda-water in the *Kabarett*? To what extent was one meant to drink for one's country? It was not as if Herr Bonhoeffer had as yet proposed further Anglo-German technological links, or even any detailed assessment of the Conference proceedings. And not a word about the Berlin Wall or any of the vital issues. Just an apparently endless recital of his wives and how they had failed him. One could get that from one's friends at home.

The *Klingelkabarett* was a long low room, decorated with silver bells bathed in a dim red light. In the middle was a little floodlit stage where a plump girl was doing a strip-tease. Theatre in the round, thought Hervey and laughed aloud. It took a few minutes to explain the joke to Herr Bonhoeffer but it went down well in the end. Hervey was pleased. He rarely made that kind of joke and when he did, it usually flopped. Hence his lack of success in the conservative clubs in his constituency.

They sat down at a large table. Several bottles of champagne appeared. A girl in a gold lamé dress came and leant on the table. Herr Bonhoeffer patted the place at his side and asked her to join them. She sat down. He put his arm around her and spoke to her very fast in a comic Berlin accent. She giggled.

'Anna, you must meet our distinguished guest, Herr Whale. He is a great British statesman.'

'*Es freut mich sehr*, Fraülein Anna,' said Hervey, reviving pre-war memories of lessons in polite German conversation in Hanover.

'Hi there,' said Anna, 'Do you know Preston?'

'I've been there.'

'You must know my cousin, Mrs Hartmann. She lives in Rossendale Road.'

'No, I'm afraid not.'

'Anna has many friends of all nations,' said Herr Bonhoeffer kissing her on the nostril.

'I get around,' said Anna.

Herr Bonhoeffer felt that the party was still not going with the requisite *Schwung*. He shouted for more champagne. In a few minutes two men in bulky, creased suits arrived with champagne buckets. They bowed in drunken imitation of two obsequious waiters. Hervey recognised them as Major McCambridge's East European colleagues.

'Ah my revisionist comrades,' cried Herr Bonhoeffer, 'how goes the Revolution?'

'The capitalists' graves are dug,' replied Plekhov. 'We ambushed your champagne in the corridor. It was all I could do to restrain Zabresti from drinking it there and then. These Poles have such a terrible passion for champagne.'

'Come and join us and then we can have some constructive East-West conversations.'

Plekhov and Zabresti shook hands very quickly with everyone at the table. Hervey felt the evening was getting out of control. On the other hand, he felt a good deal fitter.

There was nothing like champagne.

' A pleasure to see you again so soon, Mr Whale,' said Plekhov, ' and how do you find Berlin?'

' I'm enjoying my stay very much.'

' It is sad that there should be so many beautiful girls in the West and so many handsome men in Democratic Berlin ' – he blew a kiss at Anna – ' A divided city is a tragic thing.'

A photographer came up to the table and took a flash-light picture, illuminating Plekhov's mournful, pouchy face.

' In that case,' said Hervey, ' why did your friends build that hideous wall and shoot anyone who tries to cross it? Brutality is surely not the way to reunite a city.'

' Alas,' said Plekhov, refilling his glass, ' the neo-fascist militarists in the west forced us to it with their *Revanchiste* propaganda. They threatened to smash the infant DDR and destroy our beautiful socialist experiment.'

' I agree that West German pressure may have increased the tension a bit. But two blacks don't make a white, you know.'

' Neo-colonialist racialism,' said Plekhov gloomily, ' you're all the same.'

' I really don't see – ' began Hervey irritably, when Anna put a restraining hand on his arm.

' You must not try him too hard, Herr Whale. It makes him so sad. He weeps for the fate of Berlin.' At that moment, Plekhov did indeed bury his face in his hands, but whether to conceal grief or to go to sleep was not clear.

On the other side of the table, Herr Bonhoeffer and Zabresti were engaged in a trial of strength with their right hands clasped and elbows on the table. Zabresti was gradu-ally forcing Herr Bonhoeffer's forearm back. They were both flushed and grunting. Anna sat demurely between them watching the knight errants competing for her favours.

At last Zabresti succeeded. Herr Bonhoeffer's whole body keeled across the table smashing a wine glass. An ice bucket toppled over and emptied its now liquid contents onto Herr Bonhoeffer's trousers. Herr Bonhoeffer got up and began swearing at Zabresti. In doing so, he jolted the table again and some knives and forks and a few more glasses fell to the floor like a light shower after a thunderstorm. Hervey and Plekhov clutched at those champagne bottles which were not yet empty. Herr Bonhoeffer was above these petty domestic considerations.

' You cheated, Zabresti! Your arm was over the agreed line when you started pressing. A typical dirty Communist trick. I give you godless bastards a taste of civilized living and you treat the place like a pig-sty. That sort of behaviour may please your bosses in the Kremlin, but this is the Free World, not your stinking prison over there. Get out!'

Herr Bonhoeffer launched a big right-handed punch at Zabresti, who saw it coming, ducked and left the table with dignity, bowing to Anna and Hervey. Plekhov drained his glass and stood up.

' What a charming evening! I fear Comrade Zabresti and I must be going. I'm sorry it had to end so suddenly. But – *c'est la guerre* !' As they turned to go, he gave a wave, half-way between the Communist clenched fist and an operatic farewell.

But Herr Bonhoeffer did not see this graceful reconciliation of manners. The failure of the big punch to reach its target had put him off balance and he had fallen into the arms of the photographer who was replacing a flash bulb. The photographer was severely winded by the impact of Herr Bonhoeffer. This cheered Herr Bonhoeffer up. At least part of the enemy had not gone unpunished.

'My dear Hervé, I am so sorry. A most unpleasant scene. Not at all constructive. One has to watch out when these Communists get familiar. Zabresti is not a bad fellow really but he has no moral sense at all.'

Herr Bonhoeffer paid the bill plus breakages and they went outside where the government limousine was still waiting. Hervey was put beside the driver; Anna and Herr Bonhoeffer sat in the back. Turning round to ask about the agenda for tomorrow's conference session, Hervey noticed that Herr Bonhoeffer's hand was quite a long way up Anna's skirt. He now regretted that he had not taken up Herr Bonhoeffer's suggestion at dinner that a girl should be supplied for him and, if desired, for Cruddace-Smith as well. On the other hand, it had been a tiring day.

Chapter 7

Along the tenth fairway the beeches were shedding their
leaves. The heather in the rough was a dull brown. Even
the loud-voiced film producers' wives were wearing trousers
of a drabber hue. It was flannel now, not sea island cotton
against which their great thighs strained, as they played
their approach shots to the green. They swung their clubs
awkwardly as if dragging them through thick mud. The
almost ritual slowness of their swings contrasted sharply
with the volley of self-criticism, flattery and gossip which
rang out between shots. The taller wife said it was amazing
how well they were playing, seeing how stoned they all
were last night. The smaller one said: ' Stoned, Christ, I'll
say we were.' She laughed like a startled screech-owl.
' Buzzy really had a load on,' persisted the taller one. ' I
didn't think he'd get down the drive – my, what a fine
shot, Marianne. You hit that real good.'

They passed on out of sight, laying waste the autumnal
silence. Cynthia Whale, leaning on the gate-post watched
them go, and speculated idly on what depths of dissatisfaction could drive middle-aged women to such tight
trousers and braying voices. She stood irresolute, shivering

a little. The ends of her silk headscarf and her macintosh flapped in the wind. Her stockings had been splashed by the walk down the muddy path.

She looked happy. Her mouth was less pinched than usual and her eyes looked less strained. In an unemphatic way, her appearance was a tribute to Major McCambridge. He had worked no miracle cure for the affluxion of the years. But he might have put her in better shape to face them.

Cynthia smiled to herself as she turned up the hill to the house. What an absurd position one was in. They had so little to say to each other, so little in common. Their conversation was desultory but not unfriendly, springing from the same sociable motive as a non-drinker's occasional glass of sherry. They arranged to meet, they met and they parted, not before they had arranged to meet again. That was all there was to it.

She reached home at the same time as Major McCambridge and his Jaguar. He got out and they kissed – formally for the benefit of anyone who might be lurking in the dank laurels beside the drive.

' How are you then, my darling?'

' Well. And you?'

' An exhausting morning in the Boardroom. But the thought of you kept me going. You're looking very lovely today.'

' You know how much I dislike flattery, Jack.'

' My dear Cynthia, nobody dislikes it. The thicker you lay it on, the more pleased they are.'

These easy exchanges completed, they walked arm-in-arm up the stairs. They moved from their meeting into bed as smoothly as if under the directions of a time-and-motion expert.

Later, Major McCambridge explained how he had met Hervey in Berlin. They discussed Hervey with sympathy and even affection, as if he were an old gun-dog who might have to be put down. He was one of their few common topics. 'How was the poor old boy?' asked Cynthia.

'Looking a little peaky, I thought. These diplomatic beanoes are damned tough on the liver.'

'Poor thing,' said Cynthia, stroking McCambridge's compact, hairy shoulders.

She wondered in her turn about McCambridge's wife, Maisie. It seemed vaguely unfair that they should never discuss her. But then there was perhaps little to discuss. Maisie spent her nights in bridge clubs where the stakes were as high as the standard of play was low. And she whiled away her days undergoing esoteric treatment in beauty parlours. Massages, colonic irrigations, face-lifts, evil-smelling mud-packs, all were eagerly employed in the quest for change and love, but her stubby body remained obstinately immutable and unloved. Cynthia had been able to spend one enchanted night at McCambridge's apartment because Maisie had had to go down to Worthing to have her teeth sharpened.

McCambridge maintained a guilty loyalty towards his wife. He found Cynthia's interest in her lacking in taste.

Downstairs, in the front porch, Brigadier Whale was straightening his faded I Zingari tie. He rang the bell. There was no answer. Must be the servants' day out. Extraordinary what the Welfare State had reduced one to. Morale always went downhill without domestic staff. No one to keep up appearances in front of. Still even these days it couldn't be right to make one hang about outside in the pouring rain. Come on the wrong day perhaps. No, there it was in his diary. 'See Kovacs, re hurdles for Hunter

Trials. 4.30 p.m. tea Cynthia, Winkhill.' Rum business. Have a look through the windows. Cynthia might be lying bound and gagged in a drawing-room rapidly filling with gas. On the other hand, better not. It was a dangerous business for old men to look through strange windows. Women magistrates always sent those peeping toms down for years. Perfectly harmless occupation really.

The Brigadier rang again. Cynthia appeared stuffing her silk shirt inside the waist of her tweed skirt.

'Oh hullo, I almost forgot about tea. It's too awful. But it's absolutely lovely to see you.'

'Damned wet outside, you know, Cynthia.'

'I am so sorry. Come in and get warm while I put the kettle on.'

The Brigadier followed her into the drawing-room, ostentatiously shaking off the rain like a spaniel. He warmed himself with his back to the fire, rocking up and down on his toes to lull himself into a better temper.

'Well, well. All alone here, eh?'

'Yes. Hervey's coming back from his trip tomorrow.'

'I must say he's taken his time about it, at the taxpayers' expense too.'

'They're hoping for some useful results out of the conference. Apparently there's a good chance of a new agreement on those terrible tariffs.'

'Are they now? A lot of chit-chat and junketing, if you ask me. Of course I'm just an old soldier. Never could see much use in politicians. All they do is stop you getting on with the job.'

The Brigadier rubbed his hands together as if about to tackle some demanding piece of manual labour.

'I suppose someone has to do it,' said Cynthia vaguely as she left the room to get the tea.

The Brigadier looked out of the window at the rain which was now falling steadily. Two figures were crawling down the tenth fairway under brightly coloured umbrellas. These two garish beetles were followed by a pair of gaunt caddies in dirty raincoats and caps, each bent under the weight of a golf-bag. The Brigadier stared at them with approval.

At least one could still get a caddy these days. Those trolleys were so damned effeminate, like dragging a shopping-basket on wheels after you. Splendid caddie he always used to have at Gleneagles, most amusing chap. He had a great sense of pawky Scotch humour. What was he called? McIsaac, McCambridge – no, not McCambridge, he was that odd friend of Hervey's. McAughter, that was it. Wee Aughie they used to call him. ' Dinna use your neeblick like an instrument of torture, ye should strrroke the ball like a bonnie wee lass.'

What fun they had all had.

The Brigadier became aware of a strange rhythmic snoring noise in the room above. Was it some defect in the hot water system? At all events, one ought to do something about it.

He went out into the hall and called to Cynthia. There was no reply. The kitchen lay at the other end of the house, and the walls were thick.

The Brigadier slowly climbed the stairs. He tracked down the source of the noise. It was in Cynthia's bedroom. He tentatively knocked on the door.

' Who's that, darling?' said a male voice, sleepily confusing question and answer.

Surely Cynthia had said that Hervey was not back till tomorrow. He could hardly have slipped in unobserved. But if not Hervey, who? The voice was certainly familiar.

The Brigadier flattened himself against the passage wall and said 'Who's that, darling?' to himself several times. Three comatose words, not much to go on. But even so, it was clear that the voice was not Hervey's – still less George's. The Brigadier's mind began to leave its muddy moorings.

Not Hervey, not George and – moving through the respectable alternatives with military thoroughness – not of course the Brigadier himself. The answer could not therefore be respectable. Well, well. The Brigadier gave a nervous inward chuckle. Who would have thought it of Cynthia? The phrase ' a dark horse ' leaped to his mind – or was it ' a dark one '? Not surprising though. Hervey had never been much of a success with women. And Cynthia was still a fine woman. Besides, who was one to disapprove, being past all that sort of thing oneself? The Brigadier was decidedly excited. His breath shortened. He tiptoed back along the passage and down the stairs, still trying to unravel the mystery.

When Cynthia came in with the tea-tray, he was relaxing on the sofa, reading *Men and Horses I have Known* with careful unconcern.

'Ah, there you are, my dear. I was wondering where you'd got to.'

'I am sorry to have been so long. I hope you have not been too bored.'

'Not at all, not at all. Most entertaining book. Old Lambton certainly knew how to write.'

'Yes,' said Cynthia, 'I remember Harry Strachan saying it was his favourite book in the whole world.'

Harry Strachan! That was it, of course. As Strachan of the Tenth, he had been the most dashing of subalterns. The Brigadier still recalled his lissom charlestoning with adoring debutantes. And once a gay dog, presumably always a gay dog. But, good heavens, he must be sixty at least. The Brigadier cast his mind back fifteen years. How had he himself felt at that age? Desire had not then failed, but the drive to see desire satisfied had already weakened. He would certainly not have embarked on such an autumnal fling. But he was surprised that Cynthia had not been able to do better for herself. After all, Strachan was a good sixteen stone. And his face, though replete with character, was certainly not conventionally handsome. One had to hand it to him.

They chatted on across the fireplace. The Brigadier stole occasional glances at Cynthia over his tea-cup. She looked relaxed and pleasantly flushed by the heat of the fire. Or was it by the heat of passion? The Brigadier took another brandysnap to steady his thoughts.

When he stepped into his black Morris Minor, the sky had cleared. It was a fine autumn evening. The copper beeches were burnished. And the raindrops clinging to the rhododendrons glistened.

'You must come again soon. When Hervey and George are here.'

'Thank you very much, my dear. I have enjoyed it.'

The Brigadier blew Cynthia a kiss. And the little car moved slowly forward, slowly because the handbrake was still on. He remedied this and the car accelerated violently as if a booster rocket had been fired out of the exhaust pipe. The Brigadier waved gallantly as he disappeared round the bend in the drive.

The lane to Gravell village which led off the main road went straight past Colonel Strachan's creeper-clad rectory. On a puckish impulse the Brigadier stopped the car and knocked on the front door. Colonel Strachan opened it.

'Ah, good evening. So you're back then?' said the Brigadier.

'Good evening, my dear Whale. Do come in. Good to see you.'

They went into the drawing-room. Strachan poured two stiff whisky-and-sodas. They sat down.

'By the way, what do you mean by " so you're back then ", I haven't been away for months?'

Brazening it out, thought the Brigadier admiringly. 'Not even to Winkhill? I've been taking tea there and I thought Cynthia said she'd seen you in those parts.'

'No, not for two years. Nor would it have been such a remarkable journey if I had been. It's only thirty miles away, you know, my dear Whale. Not the end of the world in the age of the motor-car.' Strachan's puzzlement was turning into irritation.

'No indeed. Well, well,' said the Brigadier, ' I must have misheard what Cynthia said. Getting so damned deaf these days.' No point in overplaying one's hand. Enough to let him know that one knew too.

There was a pause.

'And what can I do for you?' Colonel Strachan asked at length, as if prompting some stumbling actor.

'Ah yes indeed,' said the Brigadier, suddenly realizing that he had no story to account for his call. ' Yes. It's – it's about the Gravell hunter trials.' Most of the Brigadier's social calls related to the Gravell hunter trials. ' I wondered if you had sent out the entry forms.'

'My dear Whale, not only have I sent out the entry forms. It was also clearly stated on your instructions, as you no doubt remember, that they were to be returned to me by October 1st. As a result of the earliness of this closing date, we have the smallest entry for years.'

'Splendid, splendid. Always just as well to double-check you know. And now that I have done so, I had better be pushing along. Please give my regards to your wife.'

The Brigadier's nerve was cracking. Strachan's bristling demeanour seemed to indicate that he had gone too far. Yet there was no way of withdrawing one's insinuations. No way for him to explain that his behaviour was roguish rather than malicious. That he only wanted to assuage his loneliness.

The Brigadier drove home. The cook had left him a cold supper in the larder. He took the supper into the drawing-room and brought a decent bottle of claret up from the cellar. He turned on the television. There was a talent competition for beat groups on the screen. The Brigadier munched his salad.

The talent competition was followed by Part Four of a series on The Coming of Automation. This episode was called Computers – The Dawn of the Super-brain. The Brigadier watched it carefully. He was partial to such glimpses into the millennium.

Mrs Strachan returned home late from the parish meeting.

'Anybody ring up, Harry?'

'No, darling. But old Whale came round. Mad as a hatter. Kept on insisting I'd been over to Winkhill today. Then he started blathering about the hunter trials and trying to teach me my job. I've never seen him so steamed up.'

'Poor thing. He must get very bored all alone in that big house.'

'Of course the old boy's a fairish age now.'

'He must feel the need for company.'

'Yes, he must be seventy-five if he's a day.'

During dinner, the Strachans watched Computers – The Dawn of the Superbrain.

'Fearful stuff,' said Colonel Strachan, 'I can't think who watches it.'

Chapter 8

It was indeed raining in Arrèche. The gutters were full
of water heavy-scented with the dust. The orange roofs of
the houses glittered while their plaster walls went grey and
blotchy. It was already dark and getting cold when
they arrived at the cottage. The maid was waiting for them.
She said the lights had fused and the water system was not
working. This had only just been installed at some expense
by Solange Lévy. There appeared to be a considerable time
lag between the fall of rain and its appearance in the water
pipes. The best minds in Arrèche had been unable to locate
the trouble. But water would definitely appear in a day or
two. Smilingly, she withdrew. She said there were some
candles in the cottage.

Except for the defective modern conveniences the cottage
had been left as Solange had found it. Writers, she said,
preferred it that way. It was a small cottage. There were
two bedrooms. George and Miriam were given the one on
the street. Ray said he and Annabel had better have the
one at the back with its fine view of hills falling away to
the sea. Ray said the mosquitoes would come in there from
the garden and they would be woken up abominably early

by the sun. In fact, the window faced south-west and was guarded by a mosquito gauze.

No candles could be found. They had some bread, tomatoes and liver sausage and went to bed.

'Come over here, darling,' said George.

'No,' said Miriam. 'I'm too tired.'

'You're like those wives in the women's magazines. After a long day's housework, I am too tired to respond to my husband's caresses. He thinks I do not love him. What shall I do?'

'Shut up,' said Miriam, sleepily turning away.

George lay awake. The rain had stopped. There was an occasional crunch of footsteps on the wet gravel of the street. A baritone voice started singing some old Basque song, softly and flat. The baritone was silent for a moment, then spat. George thought the sheets seemed rather damp.

The walls of the cottage were thin. In the next room George could hear Ray and Annabel ecstatically bouncing up and down. The bed-springs were rusty.

'No more now, Ray,' said Annabel panting. Her long black hair floated about her long naked body. The mascara around her dilated eyes was smudged, exaggerating her panda look. Ray flopped back on to the pillow and looked at his own body with critical approval. He started picking at his toenails.

'I'm getting so old,' said Annabel.

'Permit me to offer my sympathy.'

'You don't know what it's like. The hell of wrinkles.'

'Oh, lay off. Why can't you sink gracefully into middle age?'

'We've been together nearly three years now on and off. Don't you think it's time we – ?'

'What?'

' Well, one thing or the other.'

' I don't want either. But if you want to pack it in, there's nothing stopping you.'

' You know I don't want to.'

' Eh bien.'

Ray lit a cigarette casually like the amoral hero of a French film. So many girls, so many French movies and apparently so little gained. Irritation and disgust were destroying the simple joys which he had thought life's irreducible minimum. ' One has a rather amusing dinner, gets rather amusingly drunk and has sex with some rather amusing woman ' – as one companion of his youth had put it. But what if these things ceased to be rather amusing? The boredom which smothered bachelors in their late twenties so easily turned to bitterness. The acid could of course be negatived to the vegetable alkali of marriage. But was Annabel the right catalyst?

She had become the chorus in the song of his love-life. Every time he returned from some sensual excursion, she was there waiting, hopelessly lovely and hopelessly silly. Her thin body trembled with desire, the nerve-ends almost visible through her smooth skin. How could so little flesh hold so much life? Those strange, sad angular poses and those big dark eyes. Shades of old Vienna and Egon Schiele. Oh Ray darling. Darling indeed.

And in a way one shared her belief in living life to the full while one could. Yet she seemed to know so little about the world she was so anxious to experience. She was determined to be done down, to lose out. But surely the religion of failure was not Living. There was no life force in a doormat. Vitality meant success, defeating your feebler opponents, getting to the top of any tree that took your fancy.

Annabel was sobbing into the pillow and muttering inaudibly. In one of her more distinct moments, Ray heard her say, ' You just *use* me.'

There seemed nothing to be done. Ray turned over and went to sleep.

George woke to find the day already uncomfortably hot. Miriam was in a deep smooth sleep. The penalty for rousing her from it was always a spasm of bad temper blending into a day of unleavened sulkiness. He envied this faculty for total unconsciousness. He himself often spoke of sleeping like a log or being out for the count, but in fact his sleep started too late and ended too soon. On the other hand, he could not claim to sleep badly. When in bed he did eventually doze off. It was plain cooking, functional sleep rather than the licentious continental delicacy which girls seemed to enjoy. The only revenge one could take was to wake them up. But this backfired. Sybaritic sleepers seemed to feel insulted by being woken up, as if their honour had been impugned. Were their contacts with the underworld of slumber really so stimulating? When one considered the dullness of other people's dreams, the banality of their subconscious, one wondered why they did not prefer the company of the waking.

George went downstairs and out into the little patch of garden at the back. Ray was sitting on the parapet which bounded it. In the valley below, the river was still dried up. A thin stream traced an illogical course through the broad beds of shingle down to the sea, just visible through a gap in the foothills. To the right the valley widened out into a plain with neat fields of millet.

' You've heard the worst?' asked Ray. ' We've got to go up to the villa this evening. Solange is giving a frightful party for Dada and the Electric Prince.'

'Do we have to go?'

'I suppose so. It always amazes me this pressure one feels to accept invitations. We all seem to believe that we have to invent excuses if we really loathe the hosts – previous engagements and all that. Why can't one say one has no wish to go to a party at all on the seventeenth, and that, even if one did, it would not be their party one would choose?'

'Strange in that case that you're always the first to arrive and the last to leave.'

'My dear, that's just a myth put about by mothers and continued by wives. "You always enjoy it when you get there." Quite untrue. Take Solange's parties. If you sit happily by yourself refilling your glass, you are unprotected. Solange will immediately drag some drunk film producer over to meet you or some woman who wants to tell you all about her hysterectomy. That happened more when I was a medical student, of course. All the hypochondriacs in France used to confide in me. Happy days,' said Ray with a sigh.

At this moment Miriam came through the kitchen-door, sucking an over-ripe fig. She paused on the doorstep to let the sun and the sea and the foreignness of it all take their hold on her. Ray thought his sister looked sluttish. In theory he liked a high finish on girls although Annabel could hardly have been described as well-groomed. He admired the whole idea of dandyism; the social aspect he found particularly appealing. Noble was the heart that suffered silently beneath a fifty-guinea suit. His own pink shirt and tight cream linen trousers were perfectly pressed. His espadrilles were fresh. Miriam's jeans were dirty and the zip had got stuck half-way. There was a slight tear in her shirt.

George suddenly found her very beautiful. In his attempt to look detached, to show that they did not belong to one another, he let go of the stone ledge against which he was leaning and overbalanced. Miriam noticed and was flattered. She was fulfilling her role as a gamine, overwhelming with her innocent sensuality the neurotic Nordic milord. She was the life-force against which his fettered spirit was powerless.

'Christ, it's after one. I must go and see about lunch,' she said.

In the afternoon they lay down and slept in the garden. It was very hot and there was no shade. The stony patch of ground was not ideal for lying on. Even where a few blades of grass had grown, the earth was hard-packed and uneven.

As George was brushing his hair before they left for the villa, he heard the roar of a motor bicycle outside the window. He looked out. Graham Earnshaw, wearing only a crash-helmet and lederhosen, was parking the machine outside the cottage and unstrapping a khaki kit-bag from the pillion.

'Did you ask Graham to come and stay?'

'I may have said that if he wasn't doing anything else – '

'Well, he isn't doing anything else.'

'How *lovely*,' said Miram.

Graham was very pleased to see them.

'Did you get my wires, lads?'

'What wires?' asked Ray.

'Well, I sent one from London, one from Paris, I think and one when I broke down in Bordeaux. Otherwise I'd have been here days ago. But the old rattler got me here in the end and that's what counts, isn't it?'

George turned to Miriam who was lying on the bed.

'Yes, indeed,' said Ray.

'I see you're going to a party then. I'd better have a quick wash and brush up,' said Graham, making for the kitchen.

'Will it be all right bringing Graham along to the party, do you think?' asked George.

'Oh, yes, of course,' said Miriam. 'Solange always asks people to bring anyone – and they usually do.'

'Like Fred's party in fact.'

'Only in that respect. Otherwise utterly different.'

'Except that we're both going.'

'Yes.' She smiled.

It was a walk of a mile or so to Solange's villa. They went up a steep, dusty lane lined with oleanders and coarse cacti. At the top of the hill there was a high plaster wall, topped with rust-coloured tiles. The big ironwork gates in the wall were locked. Two Basques were sitting at a table by the gates. One was asleep, his head sprawled over the table; the other was just finishing a dusty bottle of red wine. He waved the bottle at them despairingly.

'*Nicht eingehen, nein,*' he shouted, sizing them up with peasant intuition as Germans.

Ray explained that they were close relations of Madame Lévy, that they had come to her party and that she would be very annoyed if they were detained.

The gatekeeper was confused. A second opinion was needed. He woke up his colleague and they whispered together, heads bent over the table. They decided to send a message up to the villa. The awakened sleeper opened the gates and strolled off down the drive which wound through a scrawny wood of pine and tamarisk.

Ten minutes passed.

'Is it always as difficult as this?' asked George.

'Solange is very security-conscious. Press photographers and so on,' said Miriam.

'But what is there to photograph inside?'

'Nothing. She just doesn't like publicity.'

The Basque returned. He flung open the gates with a flourish. He then pointed at each of the guests in turn, saying, 'ja' to each one, except for George to whom he said, 'nein'.

'Why not?' said George.

The Basque shook his head sadly as if the reasons for George's exclusion were too deep for explanation. St Peter, one felt, must have been faced with equally tricky decisions. Ray argued, but the guards were adamant. Four guests yes, but five guests no, Madame had said.

'Well, we don't want to hang about here all night,' said Graham, 'let's go in and get at the booze.'

'That's pretty bloody, considering it's your fault that we're one too many,' said George.

'All right, all right. Don't pay any mind to me.'

'I wouldn't have to if you weren't here.'

Miriam said she would stay with George. The others went in and walked along the drive. A Swedish sports car came towards them very fast, throwing up flurries of dust and stones. The car stopped. Solange leant out and greeted them. She had long yellow hair and a thin face whose harshness was alleviated by a slow smile. She was rather drunk.

'I can't stand my goddam party. I'm going down to the sea for a bit.'

'Look, Solange,' said Ray. 'One of your secret police has refused to let George in.'

'Who the hell's George?'

'He's staying with us at the cottage. He's a great friend of ours.'

' I don't care if he's Jesus Christ. He can't come in. Too many goddam *Life* photographers as it is.'

' He's not a *Life* photographer.'

' That's what they all say. Anyway, go down to the villa and have fun if you can. Hi sweetie,' Solange said, suddenly noticing Graham. ' Where did you spring from?'

' That,' said Ray stiffly, ' is Graham. He's a sculptor.'

' I like that,' said Solange, ' I love sculptors. Not like *Life* photographers.' She passed a hand over her handsome, ravaged features. She seemed to be getting drunker as the conversation proceeded. ' It's all so complicated. I don't understand it at all.' Her face sagged with exhaustion, or self-pity or both. She let in the clutch and shot off up the drive. As she went through the gates, she saw Miriam and George standing by the road. She stopped and leant out.

' For Christ's sake, go on in. One more photographer won't make any difference, I suppose.'

' Thank you very much,' said George.

They walked down to the villa. It was a plain stucco house with a few cacti around it. It was an unpretentious adjunct to the vast swimming-pool behind with its mosaic parapets and diving-boards and water-chutes. It was as if some simple living quarters had been provided for the acolytes of a splendid temple. There were two changing huts, built as miniature pagodas with bells which tinkled in the wind, should one arise. Beyond the changing huts were some commonplace formal gardens. The neatness and greenness of the vegetation argued at least three full-time gardeners. Solange's late husband, Louis Lévy, had gone in for the grand scale.

From the drive winding down above, the scene at the pool looked like the set of an epic film. Clouds had been massing in the sky. The light was artificially bright and thundery. The patterned mosaics round the pool glittered. The water had a dull sheen. Solange's guests stood in idle little groups in a variety of costume. One large man in tropical shirt and baggy shorts looked as if he were wearing a badly cut Renaissance doublet and flesh-coloured hose. A girl in tight trousers and gaudy shirt was gesturing like a novice matador. Two women in shifts were embracing in the manner of one Cimabue saint welcoming another to the ranks of the Elect. The whole party had a restless expectant air as if at any moment the director would appear with a megaphone and allot them their lines and gestures and, more important still, explain the tone and purpose of the film as a whole.

A man emerged from the group and came to meet them.

'How do you do. I am Alvise Dall'Umbria. I am playing host. Solange has gone to smell the sea air.' The Electric Prince was thin, wiry. He had large pointed ears and large dark eyes. His trim courtesy contrasted attractively with the wild melancholy which lay behind it – but not so far behind it as to go unobserved by any passing pretty girl.

'You must excuse the imbroglio at the gates. We have had these terrible photographers here all day. They upset Solange. They are doing a report for *Life* magazine – *La Dolce Vita* hits the *Côte Basque*. Rather vulgar, don't you think? Professor Stettin is also rather tired and has gone to bed. The bar is inside. Help yourself to drinks and come and meet these people.'

He took Miriam firmly by the arm and guided her into the centre of the party. Graham followed. The other three stood temporarily irresolute. As they turned to make for the bar, George saw Graham talking to a tall, blonde girl. She was already laughing in an interested way.

'Graham's a great hit with the birds, isn't he?' said George, 'I can never see why, as he's not good-looking or particularly amusing. I suppose he tries very hard.'

'Well,' replied Ray, 'that's the only quality that counts. The surface endowment for sexual success – beauty, charm, intelligence – count for very little unless they are allied to a relentless determination. One must have no false shame about lying to girls, or treating them badly, or about revealing to them one's loneliness, or one's traumatic family background. Once you have got every conceivable weapon into play, you can make any girl you like. Though to get some girls quickly, you may need money as well.'

'What,' asked Annabel, 'about love?' She had not been listening closely.

Ray was doubtful. 'Love is a great help, but again it must be allied to determination. As we all know to our cost, passive, delicate loves are too rarely reciprocated.'

'Oh, I don't know,' said George, thinking what little part he had taken in the process of going to bed with Miriam. His love was certainly passive enough, but was it delicate? Was it not just interest in a new sort of girl, a new aspect of life? But that did in itself show interest in the girl, it was not merely undifferentiated desire. What a good thing it was, as Thomas Mann had pointed out, that modern languages had only one word for all kinds of love, from the most sacred to the most profane. That way all ambiguity was resolved. The holiest love had to be physical; the sexiest encounter had a spark of *caritas*. Everybody loves a lover and I love everybody, thought George in a detached, happy way.

Ray wandered out of the bar-room in search of ice. George thought how puzzling this artificial concept of love was. It was to him a foreign language of which he thought he knew the grammar. Yet when girls spoke it to him, they invariably talked too fast for him like French taxi-drivers. 'Do you need me?' 'You treat me like a sex-machine – what do you want of me?' 'How do you feel about our relationship?' It seemed impossible to give satisfactory answers to these questions. Yet without satisfactory answers, girls burst into tears and eventually said they were very sorry but it would be better if they did not see each other any more. No doubt these dialogues, the last relics of the medieval scholastic tradition, could be avoided or disregarded by the exercise of panache.

But George had little panache.

Dancing had now started on the terrace outside. Rhythm and blues resounded through the purple darkness. George walked out onto the terrace, cradling his glass comfortably in his hand. The night sky had cleared. He lit a cigarette and watched the moon climb out of the last remaining bed of cloud. He then turned to the dancing. It was not very talented. Graham was bobbing up and down with his tall blonde. His movements were reminiscent of P.T. rather than of total rhythm. Occasionally he snapped his fingers, out of time. At the far end of the terrace, George noticed Miriam. Her long hair was swept back behind her ears. She was dancing with the Electric Prince. Dancing, it appeared, cheek to cheek. The light was not good at that end of the terrace. One could not be sure. In any case, there was no point in making a fuss. Apart from looking ridiculous one gave Miriam the chance of complaining about one's bourgeois primness. That sort of thing was the penalty for living with an uninhibited human being. All the same, inhibitions had their uses.

Graham snaked by, clapping his hands to the music.

'Swinging, eh George?'

'Yes, great.'

In the bar, Ray and Annabel were arguing.

'But darling, it's not your body. I do think you have an interesting mind.'

'No, you don't.'

'Don't be so perverse. I really think you are original. Why would I keep on with you otherwise?'

'Because you can't find anyone else.'

He walked on down the terrace. Miriam and Alvise were sitting on a stone bench at the end. His arm lay relaxed along the top of the bench, ready at any moment to obey the brain's signal and sweep down to encircle Miriam's narrow shoulders.

'Then in August I went skin diving in the Romantic with some friends,' George heard him saying.

George wondered where on earth that could be. Was it some travel agent's hyperbolic description, like the Costa Brava?

'We stayed at a little fishing-village just outside Biarritz. A very simple life but most in-vig-or-ating.' He drawled out long words with seductive Italian relish. Otherwise his English was perfect.

'Wasn't it rather cold?' questioned Miriam keenly.

'No, not at all. As warm and soft as a woman's breast, you know.' He let his lips spread into a gentle smile. 'And the underwater life, so beautiful. Imagine silvery fishes, gliding through a deep, deep blue water.'

'It must have been wonderful,' breathed Miriam. She seemed to have been reduced to a state of hypnotized imbecility after half an hour of the Electric Prince. Where was her irreverent, snook-cocking mind, her Oxfam Marxism? The education of women was clearly a lost cause.

'It was the blue of your eyes, that deep blue,' continued Alvise. This, thought George, was really too much.

'No, no,' said Miriam, meaning yes, yes. 'My eyes are more of a mud colour.'

'They change with the light like the sea. Why, hullo. It is George, isn't it?'

'Yes,' said George.

'Miriam has been telling me about you. It is so nice to have people who are so simpatico in Arrèche. So many are just scum, merely flotsam and jetsam.' He indicated the other guests with a wave. George was surprised at this class distinction within the underworld to which he had relegated Alvise.

'Miriam tells me you are interested in philosophy. I too am interested in philosophy. I think it clears the mind.'

'Of what?'

'Excuse me?'

'What does it clear the mind of?'

'That is an interesting question.'

'Don't quibble, George. I'm getting cold,' said Miriam.

'In that case,' said George with heavy menace, 'we might go home.'

'All right.'

The party was collected, except for Graham who said here was still plenty of action. He would make his own way home. The Electric Prince said he was very sorry to see them go. They would doubtless meet up again soon.

The walk back to the cottage passed in silence. When they got home Miriam made some coffee. Nobody wanted any. They went to bed, too tired to argue over the evening. George felt the first twinges of sunburn across his shoulder-blades.

He took some time to go to sleep.

Graham returned on his motor-bike at a quarter to five. He accidentally gave a long blast on the horn as he dismounted.

Chapter 9

George sat on the garden wall. It was a clear morning.
Miriam was making coffee in the kitchen. She looked pale
in the sunlight filtered through the venetian blind. Her hair
kept flopping in her eyes. She threw it back with a nervous
sweep of her hand. Graham was still asleep in the shadow
of the cottage wall. His beard jutted out of the thin sleeping-
bag. He had refused to sleep on the couch in the sitting-
room. He said he wanted to get the damp English air out
of his lungs. He was now lying in a shallow, sandy
depression in the ground like the hurriedly scratched grave
of some prehistoric warrior. It was just before nine o'clock.

George, surveying the horizon, saw a figure in dazzling
white trousers running up through the grove of stunted
olives below the garden wall. It was the Electric Prince.
George waved. Alvise Dall'Umbria doubled his speed, skip-
ping over the projecting olive-roots. He vaulted over the
wall at its lowest point and shook hands warmly with
George.

'What a very great pleasure to see you,' he said.
'Where's Miriam?'

'In the kitchen.'

Miriam came out, wiping her hands on her old quilted dressing-gown and rubbing the sleep out of her eyes.

'Good morning. You look charming,' said Alvise.

'Oh, it's you, how nice,' said Miriam.

'Look, I have brought you these flowers. How do you call them, Jonsions?'

'Gentians. You are kind.' She held out both hands, took the cluster of blue flowers and held them to her breast, inclining her head to smell them.

'I went up into the hills at dawn and saw them. They were so calm and happy up there. They reminded me of you so I gathered them.'

'You are sweet,' said Miriam, her eyes adance.

He smiled all too gravely and bowed.

'I have to go now. I must go and do some shopping. We shall meet perhaps at the races.' There were to be trotting races that afternoon just outside Biarritz.

'Yes, let's do that,' said Miriam, 'good-bye then.'

'Goodbye.'

He leapt over the parapet and jogged down through the olives to the road below where his Alfa-Romeo waited impatiently. The car roared its super-charged welcome and the Electric Prince vanished in a puff of dust.

It had to be admitted, there was a feeling of flatness after he had gone. The awakening of Graham, querulous and dishevelled, was a poor substitute. He complained of exhaustion. The Swedish blonde had been very vigorous. She had given him an idea for a sculpture.

'It's going to be vast and all smooth-welded. No more bloody nuts and bolts,' he said. 'But what can I do here without so much as a blow-lamp?' He spread his arms wide in a gesture of despair at the obstacles placed in the artist's path.

Later George and Miriam went for a walk. They passed through the village. The vegetable shop had little bunches of gentians for sale. Miriam did not notice.

They walked along a dried-up watercourse. Mangy sheep were grazing on the greener patches. An occasional fig-tree lurched out from the high bank above them, the earth washed away from its roots by the spring torrents. Further up, they met the shepherd of the mangy sheep. He was leaning timelessly on his staff watching an eagle circle in the sky. He also was rather mangy. He asked for an American cigarette. Miriam gave him a Gauloise. He stuck it behind his ear and grinned. George and Miriam grinned back. He then asked for another cigarette. Miriam gave him three more. He stuck those behind his ear too, smiled and turned away. They soon lost the murmur of the sheep-bells. There was no sound except the gravel rasping against their sandals. An untidy track cut across the watercourse. It led through a gorge to a large pool with rocks and alders around it. The pool was fed by a stream which curled round the mountain with the eventual aim of emptying itself into the big river. From the top of the rocks behind the pool, you could see the big river winding across the distant plain.

It was a sheer, hard landscape, lacking in humour or subtlety. Definite rocks and flat sky and, on the horizon, the endless banality of the sea. There was little purchase for the imagination on those sharp surfaces. But the pool was private, screened. It was lived in. There was some orange peel and old newspaper trodden into the dust. The girls of Arrèche came there in their Sunday dresses and, giggling, watched their sturdy lovers dive in chequered bathing-trunks from the topmost rock. Boys after school would swim naked in the pool, then munch grapes and compare their physiques with shouts of hoarse Basque laughter. But on this morning the pool was deserted. George and Miriam sat down on some grass, with their backs propped up against an oak tree.

' Are you very keen on the Electric Prince ?' asked George casually.

' Don't be silly.'

Miriam laughed. They kissed and rolled over, twisted together like barley-sugar. In the shade of the oak tree they made love. The morning had not yet lost its freshness. But the sun was already bright enough to dazzle the shepherd leading his tinkling flock along a bridle path far above the pool. He shaded his rheumy eyes but could not distinguish what the tiny agitated figures by the oak tree were doing. On the whole, he thought it unlikely that they were wrestling in anger, still less in prayer. He grinned and took one of Miriam's cigarettes from behind his ear.

Afterwards they bathed in the cold water. As they splashed through the shallows, the shepherd on the mountain cursed his luck. He could now clearly see two entirely naked people – gambolling. But they were so far below him that the stimulus to his senses remained purely imaginative.

' How funny your body is,' said Miriam.

' No funnier than yours,' said George.

They splashed each other and raced along the stony turf round the pool. Miriam won, as her feet were harder. They dressed and started down the track. As they came round a bend, a stretch of the main road became visible in the distance. A white Alfa-Romeo sped along it. Alvise Dall'Umbria had finished his shopping and was driving back to Solange's villa for lunch. His short black hair was ruffled by the wind, his profile was clean and straight as

his hirsute hands swung the wheel to avoid a peasant tentatively crossing the road. Alvise hooted crisply. Driving was
speed and speed was fine and good. The mountains and
the sea were fine and good too; they did not make
compromises. He rounded a corner and was suddenly
forced to slow down. A Peugeot saloon containing a fat
man with his even fatter wife was proceeding slowly in the
middle of the road. A little plastic doll was swinging about
in the back window of the Peugeot. Alvise blasted his horn
and, grazing the bank, overtook on the near side. The
Peugeot hooted but the Alfa-Romeo was already out of
sight.

Miriam saw the white streak of the car but could not
distinguish its occupant, though she imagined it to be the
Electric Prince. She also visualized the black curls ruffled
in the wind. She looked at George. He was not at his best.
One of his sandals was flapping, the armpits of his shirt
were stained with sweat and his face was red from the
sun.

Lunch was a dull meal with excessive emphasis on
tomatoes. Too much red wine was drunk and the party
climbed into the bus for the races feeling sleepy and sticky.
On the way the bus was passed at speed by the white
Alfa-Romeo, in which Solange was perched between Professor Stettin and the Electric Prince. Several of the
passengers in the bus crossed themselves.

The trotting track lay at the foot of sloping hills dotted
with orange-roofed villages. Its well-watered grass and
white rails looked artificially neat against the straggling
greens and browns of the hills.

The man at the ticket office recommended the most
expensive seats as being the only ones commanding a good
view. They bought them. Solange's party was sitting on a

grassy mound on the other side of the course. They had a rather better view. Solange had a big parasol. The Professor was reclining awkwardly at her feet. Alvise stood behind her, arms on immaculate hips. Poised for an instant against the mountains behind and the cloud-flecked blue sky, they looked like an Edwardian family group, patiently posing in front of a photographer's backdrop.

' We can't afford your posh seats, I'm afraid,' the Professor shouted across, cupping his hands to his mouth. Solange twirled her parasol.

George and Miriam went to place their bets. There was a long queue for the cheap Pari-Mutuel window. They stood behind a small man in a black alpaca jacket and a beret, carrying a shopping bag.

George said Pelota Baby was a serious sort of name for a horse. Miriam thought Quiche Lorraine sounded more romantic. George said it was a kind of cheese flan. Miriam challenged this. They reached the head of the queue and put ten francs on Quiche Lorraine. The man in the beret laughed heartily, revealing black and yellow teeth, and shrugged his shoulders to indicate his opinion of their selection in a suitably Gallic fashion. He put fifty francs on Pelota Baby.

' There,' said George, ' clearly a close student of the form.'

' Oh rubbish,' said Miriam, ' he's just a bank clerk out for the day from Biarritz. He probably had to rob the till at the Credit Lyonnais to raise the stake-money.'

' Well, you just mark my words. Pelota Baby is the form horse.'

They went back to the stand. Ray had bought a flask of rough red wine and some ice-creams, also some white sailor hats made of papier mâché. The hats said ' I'm a

Virgin Islander ' round the brim. They put them on.

The trotters swung round the bend and came into the straight, bright silks flapping and thin wheels whirring. They stood up to see better. Quiche Lorraine, driven by a bald charioteer with a great deal of elbow-work, passed the post well ahead of the field. There was a noticeable lack of enthusiasm among the crowd for the result.

'There,' said Miriam. They collected their winnings. The man at the Pari-Mutuel window said he couldn't remember such a long-priced winner in twenty years of trotting. He gave them 470 francs.

'That's what I call a working man's price,' said George. 'You are clever, darling.'

They had several drinks to celebrate. The afternoon wore on. They had some champagne. The 470 francs dwindled sharply. Annabel complained of a buzzy feeling in the head. Miriam said she felt rather buzzy, too. They retired to the Ladies.

'Seen one trotting race, seen 'em all,' said Ray.

'Miriam's feeling a bit sick,' Annabel reported on her return, ' and she says she's only had one glass of champagne, so you're not to think she's plastered.'

'The thought hadn't crossed our minds,' said Ray.

George was surprised. Miriam was so tough normally. Could she perhaps be – no, they had not known each other long enough for that, and besides, they had on the whole taken precautions. One must not fall into the delusion of supposing that one night of passion necessarily led to an eternity of shame.

The odds were strongly against it.

They left the stand and walked out to the collecting ring to wait for Miriam. On the sandy ring, horses were pawing the ground and shaking their heads, while their drivers adjusted their goggles and tightened girths. Old men in double-breasted dove-grey suits stood chatting soberly in the centre of the ring. Quiche Lorraine's bald driver was listening impassively to a small owner who seemed swamped by the enormous race-glasses slung round his neck.

In the shade of the two chestnut trees behind the ring, elegant women sat on little wooden chairs, sipping cups of tea. The chairs were as green as the grass, so that the women looked curiously as though their severely corseted bodies were floating. After the drivers had mounted, the stable-lads gathered in groups along the peeling orange wall of the stables and rolled themselves cigarettes.

The horses left the ring. And the crowd drifted back to the stadium. It was the last race, George heard the roar of the crowd, low and intermittent as the race started, but gathering strength as the horses rounded the turn into the straight, and dying to an excited buzz of conversation after the race was over. The horses came back past the ring towards the unsaddling enclosure. They were sweating lightly. The bright silks of their drivers were spattered with dust.

They stood idly for a while, watching the crowd leave the course. Graham drank some red wine holding the bottle above his head, as if squeezing a wine-skin. Solange and Professor Stettin appeared. Alvise Dall'Umbria was not with them. Solange did not look pleased.

'Solange, where's your Prince?' asked Ray.

'The little bastard sneaked off during the racing. I suppose he's eloped with your sister.'

'Miriam felt sick. He may have taken her home,' said Ray.

'How kind of him. I hope she feels better afterwards,' said Solange, savagely. 'Meanwhile, who the hell is going to take us home? Jacob, darling, do you think you could get us some taxis – I really don't like this town at all.'

The Professor padded off, espadrilles flapping. In his dirty linen suit and straw hat, he looked like a banana-planter who had gone to seed. Solange, on the other hand, was relishing the drama. Her skin shone brown and healthy in the sunlight. Her eyes were calm and blue. Even her coarse yellow hair straggled with a certain gipsy panache. She took a gulp of red wine, throwing back her head and tightening the clean line of her chin.

George leant against the peeling wall in an attitude of despair. Was his world crumbling as fast as the wall? Perhaps it was his fault. If he had surrendered himself wholeheartedly to Miriam, she might have done the same in return. This latest breakaway might be a justifiable revolt against the meaningless of their relationship. Yet surely these comments of surrender and meaningful relationships were just sentimental top-dressing. There was much more of the slave-market about the world of love than people were prepared to admit. Miriam and he had taken each other on as refreshing novelties. Now the novelty had worn off, for her at least, and normal market forces came back into play. And one could not deny that in the free market the Electric Prince would always command a higher price than George Whale. One might deplore the fact, as George did, that mere physique should count for more than moral and spiritual beauty. But the fact remained. Miriam was essentially a girl for the big league. Her egalitarian views about the ideal arrangements of society did not extend to her own daemon. After all, the gospel of individual socialism prescribed the fullest possible development of one's own personality. If this led one into a somewhat aristocratic disregard for the feelings and interests of other people, they could not really complain. They were merely casualties of one's vital exploration of human potentialities. Progress was not possible without a certain amount of emotional vivisection. But once all human ends had been harmonized, this apparent conflict would be resolved. Nevertheless, with Miriam around it was easy to guess who would be playing the leit-motif in such a utopian harmony.

George felt drained of all energy, of any wish to fight. Two taxis arrived with Professor Stettin trotting ahead of them beckoning like an elderly dragoman. The drive back to Arrèche passed in silence.

Miriam and Alvise were not at the cottage. Ray rang up the villa. They were not there either. Solange sounded already very drunk. Professor Stettin sounded worried. He detested scenes which he himself had not instigated. It was one of those affairs in which although nothing of dramatic moment had yet happened, everyone knew that things would somehow turn out badly.

Solange went upstairs to her bedroom and played Segovia very loud on the gramophone. The Professor stiffened his martini and tried to finish an article on Pre-Islamic tomb-sculpture. At the cottage, they played poker for low stakes. George won easily, fate meting out its usual trivial compensation for inflicting some more considerable blow.

Night fell and nothing happened. Eventually they went to bed, irritated and exhausted by the absence of any crisis to break the chain of tension. Just as the lights were being turned off, Miriam came up the stairs. Her shirt was torn, her jeans were dirtier than usual, and her papier-mâché hat hung askew over one eye. She looked very tired.

' Just don't crowd me,' she said, ' I'm too dead to talk.'

Nobody crowded her. Miriam saw she would have to make the running herself.

' Well, I did go off with Alvise. We went along the coast somewhere. And he kissed me and so on. That was all right. Then he said he wanted me then and there. So I said no, I was too tired, and other reasons. So he called me a bitch and said I'd led him on. And I lost my temper and said he was a crass, conceited Fascist. And I wasn't going to just because he told me to and all that bit. So he threw me out of the car and drove off. I had to walk miles before I could get a lift.' She started crying.

' I'll ring up the villa and tell them you're back,' said Ray.

' No, please don't do that. They'd want to know the whole saga and there'd be a horrible row. Let's all go to bed.'

George was much cheered up by the story. His position, while not impressive, was less humiliating than he had thought. He tried to give Miriam a tender, understanding kiss, but she strode past him to the bathroom. She was covered in dust and mosquitoes had distributed their favours impartially about her body. Part of her trek had been through marshy terrain.

Early the next morning, George and Miriam walked down to the main road below the village to catch the bus down to the coast. Miriam said she wanted to get away from Arrèche for the day to let things quieten down. The lane wound through high fields of maize. The heavy corn swung a little in the breeze. The sky was cloudy. There might be rain later in the day.

George took Miriam's arm as she stumbled over a stone. She accepted it without warmth.

Where the lane joined the main road, there was a wayside calvary. It was the usual highly-coloured figure melodramatically nailed to a dark wooden cross. A pitched

151

roof of the same dark wood protected the figure from the elements. The cross was mounted on large concrete blocks, so that it towered above the field of maize behind. A marble plaque attached to the base asked God's blessing on the people of Arrèche. The name of the local sculptor who had made it was embossed in gilt at the bottom of the cross.

As they approached the junction, George noticed that the calvary was no longer visible above the waving corn. A group of French police were standing on the road. Some civilians were chatting on the far bank, eagerly testing their nerve against the intrusion of violence into their lives. The white Alfa-Romeo had ploughed into the field, smashing into the concrete blocks and snapping off the calvary like a maize-stalk. The Christ-figure lay upside-down in a clump of grass on the bank. Alvise Dall'Umbria's head rested on the tangled steering-wheel. He must have been there for hours. The dew had soaked his blue shirt to black. The blood had run down his neck between his thin shoulder-blades. The broken glass from the windscreen sparkled everywhere. The Great Electrician had evidently ended his sport with his Prince.

Miriam sat down under some tall bamboos and wept, her head in her hands. With her bathing-towel draped across her knees, there was something biblical about her attitude. George stood awkwardly at her side.

The policemen strolled over to them and started taking their particulars. The leaves of their notebooks fluttered in the light breeze. Miriam could not immediately recall her mother's maiden name. Then she sobbed it out inaudibly. So the police made her spell it out, letter by letter. She kept her head sunk in her hands.

Two gendarmes were drawing chalk marks on the road.

The police doctor was examining Alvise's body. An ambulance drew up, siren blaring. Two medical orderlies jumped out as fast as if their task was to save a life, rather than merely to cart away a corpse. The doctor had not finished with the body and waved them away. They stood impatiently by the side of the road. The younger one rocked backwards and forwards on his heels.

The gendarmes questioned George with bland police-men's suspicion. Your name? Address? Relationship to the deceased? None. Relationship to Mlle – consult notebook – Stettin? A friend. I see.

A wave of irritation choked George. Why should he be treated like the hanger-on of some seamy underworld? What had he to do with this spoilt Italian, killed by his own stupidity? What had he to do with fast cars and high-living, with the particular mad jazz pattern in which Miriam had enmeshed him? He hated the bright sun and the barren sensuality of its worshippers; the bad temper and the violence born of rootlessness. He, George, had roots. Why should he be torn out of his baggy flannels and leather-patched tweed coat – and thrust into buttock-constricting jeans and garish t-shirts?

His place was on the springy downland of Gravell, and on the rhododendron-flanked fairways of Winkhill, and beneath the mercantile façades of Threadneedle Street. His was the old upper-middle class totem. A decaying totem, perhaps – but still richer, more varied than the hip-swinging, finger-clicking conventions of international youth.

' It's all my fault,' sobbed Miriam. ' If I hadn't been so beastly, he wouldn't . . .'

Vengeful George, last of the English Puritans, thought that it was indeed her fault – for not weighing her actions and the harm they could cause.

On the other hand, now that Alvise was out of the way, so to speak, their holiday together might begin to go better. You had to look on the bright side.

Chapter 10

The tan had not taken. George's skin had gone a fragile brown colour like someone recovering from a tropical disease. His face did not bloom with good health, it had not the sameness of properly bronzed faces. The nose was still too long, the cheeks were still too full. He looked if anything gloomier. Alvise's death had caused few difficulties. A post-mortem showed that he had been drunk at the time of the crash. Wild skid-marks a mile down the road had been identified as those of his esoteric tyres. He had perhaps tried to turn up the lane to Arrèche and had been going too fast to make it. He was driving a supercharged Alfa-Romeo, he was a foreigner. There were plenty of reasons for such an accident. Besides, Solange was in with the local police. What was the point of enquiring into background or motives? French justice might be rough but at least it did not dabble in psycho-analysis.

But Miriam had been cut up. Stricken with confusion more than guilt, she had refused to sleep with George. This access of penitential chastity meant that George had to sleep on the sofa in the sitting-room. The nights having turned cold, Graham had brought his sleeping-bag in from the garden. Graham talked in his sleep – strange, incoherent shouts of fear. These shouts were too intermittent to lull George asleep as Miriam's steady snoring had sometimes done. For the rest of the holiday, Miriam cried a good deal. So did Annabel. She and Ray were in the final round of some emotional contest whose rules and object were a mystery to them both. It had not been a happy ship.

On the whole there was a lot to be said for sitting securely in the Tube with a full office programme ahead. It was George's first day back at work. The stiff collar bit into his sunburnt neck. His mind relaxed into the unfamiliar cosmos of the *Daily Express*. He worked through the sports and feature pages. The diverse oddness of the world, magnified by the paper's individual viewpoint, encouraged contemplation. A Lincolnshire vicar had jazzed up the words of familiar hymns. ' Hail to the Lord's Anointed ' now read ' Hurrah for Him who's with it '. Did ' it ' refer to the Holy Ghost? If so, it should surely be written with a majuscule. A deaf mute had been accused of civil disobedience outside a nuclear base. When charged, it was stated that he had nothing to say. Straightforward, grotesquerie, perhaps, but another item aroused deeper considerations :

' WHAT A SMASHER
A bearded man with wild, matted hair and dressed in a white robe smashed windows of the Middle East Airlines office in Piccadilly today. He was singing and shouting.'

Just that. There was no indication that the forces of reason and order had later taken hold. No arrest had been made, the police were not anxious to interview anyone. The frivolous tone of the headline was a vain effort to reassure readers that nothing had really happened. No rational explanation was totally convincing. For example, it was improbable that the airline manager had come down from his flat above the shop to collect the milk and, unshaven, dressing-gowned, had locked himself out and lost his temper. In that case, why the *singing*?

George reached the front page. His own surname immediately caught his eye. This often happened. Usually it was in connection with Willie Whale, the comedian. Sometimes it was about the whaling industry. Sometimes it was about Hervey Whale. This time it was about Hervey. He had resigned from the government on grounds of overwork and the need to make way for younger men. The exchange of letters with the Prime Minister was more than usually dignified. Protestations of loyalty and warm regard were bandied about. The Ministry of Economic Cooperation was to be reabsorbed into the Board of Trade. But there would be a new Minister of State with special roving responsibilities. He had not yet been appointed.

The paper implied but did not state that there were spicier reasons for Hervey's resignation. The picture of him and Cynthia sitting nervously on a sofa at Winkhill did not make things any better. Why, thought George, should the note of blameless domesticity be stressed unless it was to contrast with some scandal in Hervey's private life which could not yet be revealed?

On reaching the office, George rang up Larchmont.

' I'm afraid Mr Whale is not taking any calls today. He is extremely tired.'

' It's me,' said George.

' Oh hullo,' said Hervey. ' Look, come and have a drink at the Great Northern this evening. I'll reveal all. The whole thing's gone rather wrong.'

George sat back puzzled. Evan Pratt came into the room, looking triumphant and untidy.

'Good morning, boy. Nice to have you back with us. Sorry to hear your dad's been sacked. What's the story?'

'I don't know yet.'

'Your curiosity's not insatiable enough. I've got some red-hot news, as it happens. I've just been in to see Timmy Le Mercier. He's leaving the bank.'

'You've made my day.'

'No wait. He's just come back from Downing Street. The Old man, as he calls him – interesting patriarchal survival that – has just made him Minister of State at the Board of Trade with special responsibilities for Economic Co-operation. And, if you'll pardon the expression, a life peerage.'

'Good God.'

'Exactly. But there's worse to come. I've been offered a junior partnership in the bloody bank to fill the vast hole left by Timmy's departure. I've asked for time to think it over.'

'The Marxist's last stand?' George enquired.

'I've already surrendered mentally. The money's fantastic. By the way, Timmy would like you to step along and shake him warmly by the hand.'

'The kiss of Judas isn't in it with Timmy's handshake,' said George, as he got up from his desk.

Timmy Le Mercier was standing at his office window, hands in pockets, looking out on the world of teeming bowler-hats below. As George came into the room, he swung round courteously. His moonface shimmered with elation.

'You've heard the news, George?'

'Yes. May I congratulate you?'

'Thank you. You're very kind. It's an up-and-down business, this,' said Timmy, referring to Life. 'I doubt very much whether the old man's picked a winner. I don't know much about politics. Still, ours not to reason why. A chap with business experience may be able to get a few things doing that need doing. I'm sorry about your father. He's a very good chap. It's a wretched thing to have to go over a silly little scandal like this. I hope the papers won't use it. But perhaps you'd prefer me not to talk about it at the moment.'

'If you wouldn't mind,' said George cagily.

'Of course. Now, to get back to our own backyard, you've heard we're pushing Evan upstairs.'

'Yes, very good news.'

'He's a bright boy. So that brings us to the question of your future.' Le Mercier bent his head and pressed the tips of his fingers together as if praying for guidance. 'I had a word with the other partners and we agreed that you needed rather more scope. So we're giving you Evan's job if you care to take it on – market trends, portfolio balance and the rest. You know the ropes.' Le Mercier gave a friendly smile.

George accepted the appointment and bowed himself out. In the corridor he passed Strachey, the Chief Clerk, running the other way, his spectacles gleaming with excitement.

'Good morning, Mr Strachey.'

'Good morning, Mr Whale. It's all a bit of a whirl, isn't it?'

'It is indeed.'

Timmy Le Mercier had certainly had a startling change of opinion about George's capabilities. From being an idle, insolent office-boy, George seemed to have become an embryo tycoon, chafing for lack of scope. Both images contained some degree of truth. But the real reason for George's promotion lay in the well-hidden recesses of Le Mercier's conscience. It would obviously not look good to sack the son, as well as to oust the father. Yet at the same time he had a genuinely balanced view of life. Hervey was pushed off the top of the ladder. George was thereby enabled to climb up a rung or two. It was an up-and-down business and rightly so. Only thus could talent, drive and business acumen reap their just rewards.

George tried to ring up Miriam at the Stettin flat. She had moved out of his flat in Fulham as soon as they had returned from Spain. She said she thought it better that they should not see each other for a while. There was no answer from the Stettins.

He rang up Ray at his office.

'Hullo. You don't by any chance know where Miriam is today? She told me, but I've forgotten.'

'Oh George, hold on a minute, could you? I'm on the other line. Yes, Mr Hoppington, I absolutely agree that "We Farm by Air" is a good slogan. I think it gives the fertilizer a great image. The copy's fine. All I am saying is that you cannot have it in six-point Bold. There just isn't room. If you'd used an agency, they'd have told you there wasn't room. Would you like to think again? I'm afraid I can only give you twenty-four hours. You will? I don't advise that. They'll sting you. But if you're set on it – all right then. Good-bye.

'Now George. What did you want? Oh, yes, Miriam. I'm afraid I don't know where she is. No, no idea at all. I'm sorry. I expect she'll turn up. By the way, I've got some rather exciting news.'

'It seems to be a big morning for news,' said George.

'Oh, is it? I haven't read the papers yet. Anyhow, my

news or rather our news is that Annabel and I are going to be married.'

' Ha ha.'

' That's what they all say,' said Ray, irritably, ' it happens to be true. It isn't a shotgun wedding either. We just want to get married to each other.'

' I'm sorry. I really do congratulate you. When's the wedding?'

' Soon. You must come.'

' I will.'

George looked up Graham Earnshaw in the telephone directory. He lived in a large flat in Primrose Hill. A melodious West Indian voice answered the telephone :

' I much regret that Mr Earnshaw is not at liberty to come to the phone.'

' Where on earth is he? In the bath?'

' No, he is in the studio, creating. He can't come, nohow.'

George abandoned the struggle to find Miriam and started reading some market intelligence files which Evan had given him.

Later Evan came into the office and found George staring at the wall.

' Is it a bit of a blow then, your dad being excluded from the circles of power?'

' No, not that. I'm afraid he had it coming to him for a long time. It's my own life that seems to be in a tangle.'

' Even after Timmy's generous offer of promotion? Remember what Bert Brecht said : You've no right to an interesting inner life until your outer life's O.K.'

' Yes, and you've no right to have a God until the last mouth on earth has been fed – Sartre, or so you say. Your conversation is like a peculiarly dull record that's got stuck in a groove.'

'That's the charm of it, boy. Once you've found the true Faith, you don't ever have to bother your tiny mind again. A very present help in time of trouble, ignorance and economic stress – that's Marxism for you.'

'It doesn't seem to help when she doesn't even speak to me.'

'Why should she speak to you?'

'On the other hand, why shouldn't she?'

'I imagine, because you've done her down somehow.'

'I haven't done her down. Just because she refused to go off with this Italian and he goes and gets himself killed out of pique, there is no reason for her to behave like an outraged nun.'

'Well, she doesn't love you, then.'

'On the contrary, she said it was because she loved me so much that we ought to separate for a bit.'

'Ah, she must have her eye on somebody else. She wants a breathing space to see if she can get him without putting you off. If she can, she's quids in. If she can't, you can have a great big loving reconciliation.'

'I don't think she's like that. She doesn't calculate.'

'They all do, George. They all do. I remember a little girl in Pontyborem, as wild and simple as a mountain pony. She said she came fresh to love but I knew she'd been ridden before. She was too good at it. But I believed her. We used to go for walks up Crickhowell way when the daffs were out. Then she went off with a haulage contractor from Newport. I thought –' the *hwyl* was in Evan's eyes. George rose with dignity and stalked to the door.

The telephone rang. Evan answered. It was some bird asking for George. Evan smirked.

'Hullo, darling,' said Miriam.

'Oh, hullo, where have you been?'

'Can you meet me for lunch? Bunch of Grapes, 1.15.'
'Yes, but – '
'Must rush. Byee.' She slammed down the receiver.

The Bunch of Grapes was full of journalists in sheep-skin coats and faded blondes listening to them fever-eyed. Miriam was sitting in a corner, withdrawn and pretty. Behind her head was a large mosaic depicting scenes of viticulture. Great bunches of grapes exuberantly spilled over the borders of the scenes. In one section, a slim young man – not unlike Ray – was chasing a naked girl along a river bank. The young man was wearing a voluminous toga which would have hampered most men in the chase. But George reflected, it would not stop Ray any more than the cold mists of a Winkhill October had prevented him from bundling Annabel behind a gorse bush.

Miriam seemed pleased to see him.

'I thought we ought to have a little talk,' she said.

'Why? What about?'

'Us, you know, the way our relationship is – is going.'

'Yes?' said George, turning to elbow his way to collect two plates of steak and chips from the bar.

'Well, don't you think we're losing one another? I mean, we've got to be frank about this, haven't we?'

'I suppose so,' said George, dexterously yanking one of the plates out of range of a gesticulating sheepskin-jacketed arm.

'You see, I'm not sure that I love you enough. It's no good lying to myself about it. I don't know how you feel. But I get the impression that it's the same with you.'

'What makes you think so?'

'You're cooler somehow. You don't cherish me so much.'

'I'm not, I do. It's just that I'm bewildered. I don't know what you're up to.'

' Oh, George,' sadly shaking her head. ' We don't communicate much, do we? You never tell me what you think.'

' Because I don't know what I think.'

' You must know if you feel strongly. You would know if you really loved me.'

' Perhaps. But perhaps not. I've never been certain about anything since I thought Angers was going to win the Derby – and he broke a leg at Tattenham Corner.'

' Don't take refuge in flippancy. You're so scared to reveal your emotions. Don't be so English.'

' I am English.'

' I suppose you are. That's the real trouble. That's why you didn't like Arrèche.'

' Did you?'

' Oh, for a week or so, it's great. The sun, new people, nobody bugging you, trying to make you do things you don't want to do.'

' What about the Electric Prince?'

' That's a beastly thing to say.'

' And what about Graham – does he count as an amusing new person?'

' I'm very fond of Graham. Anyway, he's off to America next week. He's going to be Resident Creative Professor of Sculpture at the University of New Mexico. Don't you think that's marvellous?'

' Marvellous in every sense of the word.'

Miriam leaned forward earnestly. Clearly, the crucial question was coming up.

' Didn't you admire Solange even? Didn't you *respect* her?'

' Yes, I did like her. I'm not sure about respect. What do you mean exactly?'

' As a person. She's so honest.'

' I see that. Where is she at the moment?'

' Oh, still out in Arrèche. She'll sit there until the rain and the Pernod get too much for her. Then she'll go to London or Paris, and pick up some dead-beat middle-aged writer. Hang around pubs like this or cafés in Montparnasse. Then, when spring comes and the writers are exhausted, she'll go back to Arrèche – and wait for the summer crowd to arrive.'

' It's one way to live.'

' But she doesn't pretend. That's what I like.'

' Isn't the whole thing a bit of a pretence?'

' Oh George, you don't understand. She's so *good*.'

' No, I don't understand. Does she help refugees or fallen women or something? How is she helping the revolution along?'

' Don't be silly. Not good in that way. She's had such an unhappy life. Being married to that horrid old man – '

' Who left her a million and a half.'

' That's more of a hindrance than a help. It makes everything so false.'

' It might make the middle-aged writers a bit truer.'

' Why are you being so bloody to me today? I wanted to have lunch with you so you could be nice to me.'

The pub was getting hotter. Condensation formed on the windows. Outside the sky darkened. One of the journalists half-tripped over Miriam's bag. He smiled apology through his taut lips. Miriam's eyes brightly signalled forgiveness. A spark of sexuality flashed through the muggy atmosphere. The journalist said:

' Sorry, luv.'

George said he had better be getting back to the office. Miriam said she was sorry he was in such a bad temper. George said he was not in a bad temper.

Miriam put on her donkey-jacket briskly, shrugging off George's offer of assistance. But as he pulled back the door for her, she smiled at him, as if their bickering had been an act put on to deceive the paying customers. He smiled back and his lips blew her a sentimental kiss. As they stood on the pavement, she reached up for his head with both hands, like a child pulling down an orange from a shelf, and kissed him on the mouth. Then she stalked off down the grey street, swinging her bag and shaking her hair free from her coat collar.

George waited at the bus stop, stamping his feet against the cold. He thought of Miriam's body. Then he thought how he didn't really like her much. Then he thought of her body again.

Chapter 11

The Great Northern Hotel was at its best on an autumn evening. The gathering fog and darkness outside contrasted strongly with the apparently secure grandeur within. The echoing spaces and the vast pillars provided a reminder of a more ordered age that was both ironic and comforting. The Great Northern had at the same time the restlessness of all railway hotels. Businessmen in overcoats sat at the little tables in the lounge with brief-cases on their knees. The tables themselves were littered with brown trilbies and large whisky-and-ginger-ales. Every now and then, one of the businessmen got up, gathered his worldly possessions and hurried off to answer the summons of time. The others glanced at him without interest.

Hervey Whale was more relaxed. He had got rid of his coat and luggage and was smoking a cigarette in the corner of the lounge. He had looked through the evening paper but had found nothing new about himself.

'Well, George, it's difficult to know where to begin. I'd better show you the photographs first.'

He took a couple of magazine photographs out of his brief-case. He handed them to George furtively as if they were pornographic pictures the mere possession of which carried heavy penalties. The first one showed Hervey sitting at a table with an excessively made-up woman, apparently in a night club. She had her arm around him. He was looking into her eyes with an expression of surprised delight. The second photograph showed Hervey and another man grasping champagne bottles, as if to threaten a fat, florid man who was embracing the woman from the first photograph. There were captions under the photographs in German.

' They are cuttings from a West German magazine,' said Hervey. ' The woman is apparently a well-known prostitute. The fat man is Bonhoeffer who resigned from the Federal Ministry of Economic Co-operation while you were away. The reasons for his resignation were not given. In fact he had been sleeping with the woman who is also an agent for the East Germans. Plekhov, the other man holding a bottle, was her contact, as well as her lover. He has now been thrown out of West Berlin, and the trade mission of which he was head has been wound up. But not before he had obtained a good deal of useful information.' George felt as if he were listening to the synopsis of an operatic plot, whose improbably complicated twists and turns had to be squeezed into the scanty libretto of the photographs.

' Are the photographs genuine?' asked George.

' In a way.'

' Then how – '

' Well, you know how it is in night clubs. Things get out of control. I can't quite remember why Anna had her arm round me. But there is a perfectly straightforward explanation of the second photograph. Bonhoeffer had been playing some childish game with another East German. You can just see the top of his head poking out from under the table – there. As a result, the table had been upset and Plekhov and I grabbed the champagne bottles to prevent them being spilled.'

'It doesn't sound terribly convincing.'

'I assure you it is true. But that is not the point. It is obviously unfitting that a British Minister should be seen apparently *carousing* with a German counterpart who is drunk and indiscreet and with two Communist spies – three, if you count Zabresti. I believe he has been expelled too. So you see the P.M. had no alternative but to call for my resignation.'

'I do see.'

'Not that he didn't want to get rid of me in any case.'

'No.'

'I thought you ought to know the full story which must of course remain entirely confidential.'

'Of course. What are you going to do now?'

'Well, I've had a bit of luck.' Hervey's face resumed its usual expression of unshakable optimism, that Micawberism which seemed to keep politicians going. 'Jack McCambridge has got me a directorship in one of the big Lancashire building societies. I'm taking the train up tonight to meet my co-directors. Pretty quick work, don't you think? He's a very good fellow, really, old Jack.'

'He must be,' said George.

'Then, of course, I shall continue as a back-bencher. So, what with one thing and another, I doubt if we shall starve. I'm feeling rather resilient now that I've shed the burden of office.' The memory of Bonhoeffer's emphasis on the quality of resilience pleased Hervey. By showing resilience he felt he had triumphed morally over the cause of his political downfall. Besides, there was a certain sense of genuine relief in no longer having to pretend to be a figure of consequence, to be important. But the itch for that importance would undoubtedly return, and return before one was ready for it.

The withdrawal symptoms were quite as painful as those of alcohol.

'Anyway,' said Hervey, ' I'm very glad that Timmy Le Mercier has got the new job. A very able chap. By the way, how are you getting on at the bank? We must have a talk about that next week. Well, I must go and catch my train now. Above all, don't worry. Your mother's taking it very well. I think she's rather relieved in some ways. As you know, she isn't much of a one for official life.'

Hervey bustled off to collect his luggage. George went to telephone Miriam; he tried all the numbers he had tried in the morning, again without success. Only Ray was in. He said being engaged was already proving quite a strain. He was dining with Annabel's parents that evening. The thought of having to go to dinner at that house and watch Mrs Meyer's breasts wobbling at least once a month for the rest of his life was already beginning to appall him. George lost interest and put the receiver down before Ray had finished speaking.

It was just possible that Miriam might be at Winkhill, though this was unusual during the week. He rang Pontrilas. There was no answer. Professor Stettin must be struggling through some local cocktail party. Well, there was no harm in going down there. He could go and stay at home. Besides, the chase had now taken on an obsessive quality. He did not know what he would say to Miriam when he found her, or whether indeed he wanted to find her. But he wanted to resolve his uncertainty.

He got a taxi outside the Great Northern Hotel and took a cold, slow train from Waterloo. The sky was frosty and clear as he walked up the lane to Pontrilas. The Professor came to the door, coughing.

'My dear George, what a surprise. Come in.' He led George down the corridor which led to his study. He looked much older. Shuffling along the dark passage in his slippers he bore a slight resemblance to Mr Karopoulos, the weary landlord of Fred's flat. There was an air of neglect and loneliness about him. 'I expect you're looking for Miriam.'

'Yes.'

'I'm afraid she's not here. However, she left me her telephone number. It should be here somewhere.' He rummaged among the chaos of letters, bills, books propped open and paperweights on his desk. 'Here it is, Camden 3124.'

George dialled the number. Miriam answered.

'Hullo, darling. This is George.'

'Oh, hullo.'

'I very much want to see you.'

'I think it's better not, really. We'd get confused again.'

'I'm pretty confused already. Where are you, please?'

'If you don't know where I am, how did you manage to get hold of me?' Miriam sounded cautious.

'Your father gave me your number.'

'I'm staying with a friend.'

'What friend?'

'Do we have to go into all that?'

'What do you mean "all that"? It's just a question of giving a name.'

'George, do you swear you don't know? You're not just playing with me.'

'Of course I don't know.'

'Then I won't tell you,' said Miriam, delighted at the brilliance of her diplomacy.

'Why not?'

'Because it might hurt you.'

'I'd rather be hurt than driven mad by this double-talk. I suppose it's Peter van Aalen,' said George, un-covering the suspicion of humiliation that had been lurking in his mind for some time.

'There, you *are* hurt.'

'Of course I'm hurt. What do you expect?'

'Promise you won't do anything silly,' said Miriam, now in top form.

'I've no intention of doing anything silly. I can't even think of anything silly to do.'

At the other end of the line, George could hear in the background a guitar playing 'Careless Love'.

'I do hope so,' said Miriam. 'Please, please don't feel bitter. I mean it had to happen in the end. And in a little while, we can perhaps be friends again, who knows?'

'Who knows indeed?' said George enigmatically. He put the receiver down. Jacob Stettin stopped his pretence of dallying with the papers on his desk and looked up with sympathy.

'No good?'

'No. It seems to be over.'

'I'm sorry. Though if you will forgive me the hindsight, I never thought it would work. I'm only surprised you stood it as long as you did. You're not right for Miriam. Nor, for that matter, is Van Aalen. But he'll do for the moment. I only hope my son Raymond will manage to stick with Annabel Meyer – though I rather doubt it. We are some-thing of a divorcing family. Look at poor Solange – she can't stick with anyone. Lucky for her old Lévy died when he did. She was more or less on the point of leaving him – and that would have meant no money.'

George said that he ought to be pushing along.

'You can't stay for a drink? How sad. One gets rather bored with only Grünwald for company – not such a good painter as I used to think. But there, one must not carp. One's job is to create enthusiasm, not to dampen it.'

He showed George out and stood in the doorway waving, as George hurried out of the front gate.

Larchmount was ablaze with lights, as he came up the drive. McCambridge again? His mother would normally be in bed reading at this time.

His mother and McCambridge were playing draughts in the drawing-room as George came in. The gramophone was belting out Strauss waltzes. The fire was crackling in the grate. A cosy scene of Winkhill domestic life.

'Ah, George, what an unexpected pleasure,' said McCambridge. 'I just popped down to see what I could do. And your mother has very kindly given me a delicious dinner. And she's even offered me a bed, which I have gratefully accepted. I don't think there's any danger of scandal with an old hasbeen like me, ha ha.' His check suit was beautifully cut.

'Well,' said George, as he kissed his mother, 'I suppose there's so much scandal in the family that a little more will make no difference.'

'Quite so,' said McCambridge stiffly.

'Jack has been so kind,' said Cynthia. 'Have you heard about the building society?'

'Yes, I have. That was kind of you.'

'No trouble. Always glad to help.'

And it would help McCambridge's own schedule too, thought George. With Hervey up in the North, say, one night a week, McCambridge would be able to enjoy a prolonged tumble with Cynthia, instead of having to fit in a hurried hour of pleasure at the end of a long day.

George went into the kitchen to make himself a cheese sandwich. He rummaged for the breadknife. At the back of the cutlery drawer, he noticed an old piece of bread, hard and dusty. Through the dust, a reddish smear of jam glinted. George was consumed with self-pity. The world was a hard place, divided into the destroyers and the destroyed. Either, like Miriam and Jack McCambridge, you hacked your way with rough assurance through the undergrowth of the heart. Or, like George, your trousers were torn off by the first barbed wire fence.

'Well, George, and what did you think of our company meeting?' asked McCambridge.

'Not bad. I didn't find your colleagues very inspiring.'

'I agree. Though of course we mustn't talk out of school, I do feel they need a bit of a shake-up. I hope to be able to give a modest shove myself.'

'And as for your chairman – '

'Ah, poor Eric. Not the man he was, I fear. We can't hope to have him with us much longer.' McCambridge's elegy barely concealed a cheerful certainty as to the identity of the next chairman. 'Very good man of business in his day, you know. Two wives and the horses finished him off.'

'He didn't strike me as a reckless punter.'

'Certainly not. Sweated blood at the thought of risking five bob each way. No, he had a string of horses himself. Even a small stud at one time, I believe. Ruinous expense as I know to my cost.'

McCambridge laughed indulgently at his own fecklessness.

'I didn't know you were a racing man.'

'Got four beasts down at Sarsen Lodge,' said McCambridge, his eyes alight with love. 'A couple of young hurdlers. A competent though elderly handicapper who helps to pay the stable bills. And a beautiful little three-year-old filly, so far unraced. She moves like Pretty Polly, but there's still a doubt about her soundness. I was so excited when I bought her that I put my lighted cigar into my pocket and ruined a pair of new trousers.'

The alert wariness had left his chiselled face. He was talking, rambling rather, like a child recalling the events of a happy day. The artifice fled from his eyes.

'I'm going down to see them working tomorrow morning, George. Would you care to come? Wonderful, dawn on the downs, very crisp.'

'Unfortunately I've got to work myself.'

'We'd be back in London by half past ten or so. We could ring up from the Lodge to say you'd be a few minutes late.'

'I'm sure George would love to come,' Cynthia said as if she had made a long study of the topic and suddenly stumbled on the answer.

'Yes, I would,' said George rather annoyed.

'Very well then. We'll start at seven and have a spot of breakfast there.' McCambridge was his old brisk, guarded self. 'Time for Bedfordshire then, I think.' He used the squireish archaism self-consciously.

He kissed Cynthia on the cheek. George stood behind, him, as if queueing for soup. His mother smelled vaguely both of whisky and scent, in a combination so permanently her own that it always evoked his childhood.

'Good night dear,' said Cynthia. 'I'll show you to your room, Jack.'

The procession of three straggled up the stairs. George said good night and went on up to his own room on the second floor. Would they tonight, George wondered? Probably not, considering how creaky the passages were. Besides, even his mother, scarlet women though she might be, would hardly dare with her only son innocently sleeping above her.

As George sat in bed, browsing in the History of Merchant Banking, he listened for goings on downstairs. He heard only the familiar sound of the wind in the pines at the edge of the third fairway and the occasional rattle of trains passing through Winkhill Heath. Miriam already seemed a distant memory.

He awoke to find the muscular hand of Major Mc-Cambridge shaking his shoulder. He looked alert though dawn had not yet broken. Unlike Timmy Le Mercier in many ways, his square face had the same pink patina of success.

'Morning's at seven, the hillside's dew-pearled, the lark's on the wing, the snail's on the thorn,' chanted Major McCambridge.

George stared. He did not feel too good.

'Only poem I know. God's in his Heaven, all's right with the world,' said McCambridge hurriedly, as if to complete the recitation would explain it away.

George got out of bed and brushed his teeth. McCambridge paced round the room, peering at school photographs, scanning the bookshelves, picking up the ornaments on the mantelpiece.

'Nice room, this,' said McCambridge finally. His words seemed to put a precise valuation on the room and its contents.

They tiptoed downstairs and out of the front door.

A grey dawn was breaking over the rhododendrons. The third fairway sprawled away down the hill to the left, a ghostly silver-meadow, dew-pearled as Major McCambridge had promised. The Major's Jaguar crouched on the frost-dusted gravel like a sleeping animal.

'Hop in. We'd better get a move on.' McCambridge's polished brogue hit the accelerator. He drove with immense concentration, frequently fiddling with knobs to adjust the heater or the demister. Soon it was light enough for him to turn off the headlamps.

They were passing through the sandy heaths of East Hampshire. The mist was quickly lifting off the tops of the pines. The familiar outlines of distant hills and housing estates grew sharper.

This was the way to Gravell. The sun came out over Basingstoke by-pass.

'It's going to be a fine day, but there's a thin wind,' said McCambridge with a discerning sniff as he opened the window for air and turned up the fur collar of his overcoat.

They moved into softer, richer country. The shallow, trout-happy River Test wandered to and fro across the undeviating line of the main road. Chalk scars showed on the low hills. Every few miles there seemed to be a military camp. Some were deserted. Others still had khaki lorries drawn up in rows and white goalposts on the football field. Even they had an air of complete desolation. Little alder-shoots were already growing in the cracks in the concrete of the parade-ground. Further on, a beech avenue pursued its pointlessly straight course over the horizon. They came to Stonehenge. The stones were huddled together behind the encircling barbed wire. One of the megaliths was being lifted into its old position and was still gripped by ropes and scaffolding. The underside was earth-brown in contrast to the blueish-grey of the other stones. The asphalt car park and weatherboard attendant's hut formed a drab counterpoint on the other side of the road. The ensemble was not unlike one of the deserted army camps.

'Your Dad really did get himself into quite a mess in Berlin, if you don't mind my saying so, George,' McCambridge suddenly said.

'It certainly looks like it.'

'I feel rather guilty. I should have warned him about those two Commies. All right to do business with, but I wouldn't care to go drinking with them. Anyway, he must have known he had to watch out when he went out on a jag with old Bonhoeffer. And that whore, what's-her-name – Anna. He really oughtn't to have got mixed up with them, you know. Of course it's easy to be wise after the event.'

'Yes.'

'But he should have smelled trouble. That's what you need in public life – a nose for trouble. I've got it – hundreds of people have – but I don't think Hervey has, though he's got every other virtue in the book. Still, he might have quite a bit of fun with that little Building Society I got him on the board of. Not a big one, but plenty of scope for growth.'

They reached Sarsen Lodge, a long white house with stables at the back sheltered from the wind by a cordon of fir trees. As they arrived, the horses were already jogging out of the stable-yard, half-slipping on the cobbles. The stable-lads were muffled up to the eyebrows and the horses were well-blanketed. McCambridge introduced George to the short, leathery trainer. They walked out of the back of the stables up the hill to the gallops – a mile and a half of downland turf marked by little, wind-blown box-trees.

The sun was bright now, but it was very cold. Mc-Cambridge and George gulped coffee from the trainer's Thermos. The horses were out of sight in a dip in the gallops. George watched some plovers on a nearby strip of fresh plough, bobbing their sleek, crested heads in search of food. Occasionally they made short flights over the plough, mournfully flapping their outsize wings as if to complain about the cold.

The trainer was explaining why the better of McCambridge's two hurdlers had not won its last engagement.

'Yes, Jack, I grant you he was very reasonably weighted, but he needed the race.'

'So you didn't have a go. But I thought we agreed – '

'I won't say we didn't have a go. We just didn't push him. He was blowing like a steam engine when he came back. I promise you he'll be plumb ready next time.'

'I'm looking forward to the day when one of my horses is ready to win.'

They laughed.

The first lot of horses came into sight. These were the older flat-racers, the younger ones being exercised after breakfast when it was warmer. They cantered along easily, just keeping in trim during the winter in order that their joints might not stiffen up and that they be less prone to the endless list of equine ailments. The trainer pointed out a big, strong colt with a neat stride.

'He's my great disappointment this season. He should have won at both York and Newmarket, but Maguire never brought him up at the right time. That boy has got no idea at all about riding a finish. Then the horse got a knock at Ascot. Nothing wrong with him, but it made him nervous and he won't run with the bunch. You lose a lot of ground going the whole way round on the outside rails, you know. But we're going to get him right next season.'

' He looks like a good cup horse,' said McCambridge.

' He should be. He's by Alycidon out of a French staying mare,' said the trainer.

He picked up a worn, leather-covered megaphone and shouted at a pink-faced stable lad cantering by on a bay colt.

' That's horseflesh you're kicking, boy, not a bloody football. Stroke the animal, don't pummel him.'

The boy did not hear, and dug his heels in harder. The trainer cursed and shouted to the boy to come back. The boy turned round, leaning forward anxiously in the saddle. The trainer's rage was carried away on the wind. George watched his spare, angry gestures, hampered by his trim overcoat.

' Smart lad, Dick Bawden,' McCambridge whispered in George's ear. ' When he was a jockey, he hardly ever got a decent ride. And when he did win a good handicap, he'd lose it all betting. But he certainly had a way with women. That was how he got set up as a trainer, you know. After Dick won the Eclipse on Slipperillo – one of those smart fillies of old Fogdale's – Fogdale gave a big dinner to celebrate. Well, Dick asked to be excused, because he was tired and he had to go up on the sleeper to ride at Ayr the next day. And Molly Fogdale said she didn't care for that sort of thing – racing men getting plastered together – so she was going to stay upstairs in their suite. Then of course after dinner, they all wanted to drink a toast in the Eclipse Cup. So Fogdale went up to fetch it. And what did he find but old Dick wearing nothing but the Fogdale racing silks – orange diamonds with the black Maltese Cross – riding astride old Molly who was mother-naked and shouting " giddy-up there ". And that was in the sitting-room, mark you – they hadn't even bothered to go to bed and lock the door.'

'What did Fogdale do?' asked George.

'Oh, he shouted, "what the hell are you doing in my racing colours, Bawden?" Anyway, he took a fancy to old Dick after that. He was a bit past that sort of thing himself, you see, and Molly needed regular poking to keep her quiet. So he set Dick up here at Sarsen and Molly used to come down for week-ends. Very satisfactory arrangement, worked for years. Nice old boy, Fogdale. Dead now, of course. But Dick's a good trainer.'

A coarse world, thought George, as he saw the pink-cheeked stable lad trot off in tears after his rocket from Bawden. But a world where discipline and authority were still accepted. The lad took orders from the trainer who took orders from the owner who took orders from his wife or lover. Each had his place, though it might not be a comfortable place. There the idle mind could rest, never faced with anything more complex than blood lines or the daily double. There the educated heart would be called on to feel affection only for a trim filly or a brave colt. And only horse-doping would arouse real moral revulsion.

In his dreams, the racing man saw only bright-shirted jockeys mounted on gleaming horses eternally galloping across springy downs dripping into cloud-fleeced blue horizons. It was a world of clear colours and firm lines like the pictures in medieval books of hours. The world of a happy child – absorbing, secure, disturbed by no larger questions of man's purpose.

The second batch of horses came past at a good gallop. McCambridge complimented Bawden on the appearance of his two hurdlers. The trainer gave a thin proud smile. The end of his nose was red with the cold. The horses came back. Blankets were thrown over them again. The lads took them back to the stables, each lad riding one horse and leading the other. As they strung out along the path leading down to the stables, they got out of sight of the trainer. The lads rode a little more casually now, one hand on the hip with the elbow thrown out sideways in an artificial swagger. A joke about the breasts of Bawden's daughter passed down the line through the crisp air.

' She ought to play *water*-polo, then she could use 'em as mucking water-wings.' Cold lips stretched in laughter. The sun sparkled on the slate roofs of the stables below, still wet with dew.

George and McCambridge followed the trainer down to a quick breakfast of scrambled eggs and kidneys in his parlour which smelled of dogs and leather. George was two hours late for work.

Chapter 12

The unremarkable life of Brigadier Whale had drawn to an unremarkable close. The second day's shoot of the year at Gravell had taken place in a thunderstorm. The Brigadier had contracted pneumonia. His resistance had not been strong. He had now gone to face his final Commanding Officer.

The funeral was well-attended. The Brigadier might have been a foolish sad old man, but he had always been agreeable. As melancholy and to some extent senility had overtaken him, he had never lowered his standards of courtesy. And, George reflected, if it was as easy to become sadder as it was difficult to become wiser, it was never easy to stay agreeable.

The church was a simple modern structure of prestressed concrete. It had been built for the workers in the new plastics factory at Gravell St John. Gravell old church had long become a barely picturesque ruin. The Brigadier had conceived it as his duty as director of the plastics firm to attend their church parade. He rather liked the bright stained glass representing various stages in the manufacture of plastic. Anything which aggressively labelled itself as modern usually won his approval.

Everything went well. Hervey and Cynthia looked both dignified and, for different reasons, fit. Hervey was particularly exhilarated by the reception he had got from his new colleagues in the building society. They seemed somewhat puzzled as to why Hervey was joining them but were pleased to have him. Major McCambridge represented high finance, Timmy Le Mercier, the Government, Colonel Strachan, the distilling industry. Mr Hoppington spoke for fertilizers. It was a distinguished company. Snowy Kovacs and Hatchett, the two keepers, performed their duties as pall-bearers with competence. There had been some question as to whether the weight of the coffin might not put too much strain on Hatchett's internal organs and so cause yet another recurrence of his rupture. But, with his sense of the dramatic, Hatchett had protested that he would stick by the Old Master to the last.

The congregation left the church. It was raining hard. Men from the factory were hurrying back for lunch to the caravan site on the other side of the road. They had thrown yellow plastic macintoshes on over their blue dungarees. They were wearing flat caps. The funeral procession presented a striking contrast – black umbrellas, black tail coats or overcoats, black top hats. It was a dramatic confrontation between the boss class and the workers.

The procession walked self-consciously along the middle of the road to a muddy field where the cars were parked. A few of the older workers removed their caps. Two youths grinned. Major McCambridge glared at them. He turned to George.

' No respect, no respect at all these days, George.'

' I suppose not.'

' You know, I liked the old boy. Sorry to see him go,' said

McCambridge, as if justifying his old-fashioned attitude of respect. ' Had his innings of course ' – putting, in all fairness, the other side of the case.

The motorized cortège proceeded up the drive to the house. The pace was respectfully funereal. The rain beat against the window panes of the compact Victorian house. The brickwork was already washed to a deeper red. In the drawing-room the lights were on. It was a dark day.

Cynthia was handing out glasses of sherry. The guests drank with restrained greed. The funeral had placed its usual strain on decorum. How could one keep up the pretence of a minor social rite amid the passionate talk of sure and certain hope? So many unseemly emotions were aroused. The body of an old man had been shut in a wooden box and lowered by thick ropes into a hole in the dark, wet earth. There was nothing intangible, nothing synthetic about that. The most reassuring mind could not easily escape into abstraction.

Major McCambridge said, ' It was a fine funeral. Pity the weather wasn't better.'

Colonel Strachan said, ' The weather always breaks at just about this time of the year down here. We're in for a few days of this, I'm afraid.'

They looked out of the window at the sheet of rain, grey against the rhododendrons. Thicker drops of water were massing down the veins of the black-green leaves.

Cynthia said. ' Your tail-coat's getting a bit tight across the shoulders, George.'

' It is a bit tight,' said George, ' but I don't think it's worth getting a new one.'

' No, I don't think it's worth getting a new one. You wear it so rarely.'

' This outfit's good for a few years yet.'

Timmy le Mercier looked from George to his mother and back again. His face glowed with its usual expression of bland interest.

'We're very pleased with George just now, Cynthia. We may even keep him on for a week or so.' Timmy Le Mercier smiled a little, to indicate the degree of amusement appropriate to his listeners. George and Cynthia smiled a little too.

'Oh, I'm so pleased to hear that. George tells us so little about his work.' Cynthia smiled again and moved off with the sherry decanter.

Le Mercier moved closer to George and put his arm on George's shoulder. They must be going to talk business.

'Tell me, George, what do we pay you now? I've been so out of touch recently, what with one thing and another.'

'Eleven hundred.'

'Only eleven hundred? My goodness me, I think we can do better than that. You really should have put in for a rise earlier, you know.' Le Mercier patted George's shoulder in time with his concluding words.

'I did,' said George.

'Did you now? Lost in the post, I expect. You know what the red tape is like in the office. I think old Strachey will strangle himself with it one of these days. But, as I say, I think we can do you a little better now that you'll be taking on Evan's job. What do you say to eighteen hundred?' He looked into George's face, appealingly, as if imploring him to accept this offer, inadequate though it might be.

'I'd prefer two thousand.'

'Ah, wouldn't we all, wouldn't we all? Well, I'll see what I can do, George. But of course I don't have any official say in the matter now that I've left the Board.

Besides, two thou' is rather above the going rate for your sort of position, you know.'

' I think that's considerably less than Evan was getting, in fact.'

' Ah well, don't let's haggle about it, George. Perhaps I shouldn't have brought the subject up, the occasion being what it is. Let's have another chat some other time.' Le Mercier was almost irritated.

As he turned to refill his glass, George felt pleased with his firmness. The value of his labour had increased spectacularly. But how and why? Timmy Le Mercier would have been able to explain, had he been prepared to reveal the workings of the competent mind that lay deeply entrenched behind his bland manners. Major McCambridge would have recognised the fact too – would have ' smelled ' it, though he could not have explained it.

But there it was. George had suddenly become more valuable. There were obvious contributing factors – Evan Pryce's elevation, Le Mercier's need to make some pro-Whale gesture, the lack of anyone else in the office who was familiar with its operation at the clerical level.

The laws of the free market had woven these and other circumstances too minute to be worth identifying into a new pattern. Supply had responded to demand. George's marginal wage cost had risen in parallel with George's marginal utility.

These laws were thought of as efficient and useful by those who profited by them. And harsh and inhuman by those who did not. But they were as morally neutral as the law of gravity. Miriam's rejection of George was no more to be blamed than her love for him was to be praised. She had only behaved as she always behaved, with a mixture of impulse and self-interest, which though only half-conscious brought results. And, in a quieter key, George's behaviour had echoed hers. He had wanted her, been surprised and delighted that he could have her, irritated and hurt when the affair ended. But there was no question of any dogged attempt to recapture, no despairing pursuit.

But if you behaved only as you were likely to behave, how difficult to pretend that you were taking moral choices, or even choices at all. Was man still to be ruled by a necessity which, if not grim, was sadly foreseeable? Could you not occasionally surprise yourself?

All the lights went off in the dining-room. The wiring at Gravell had always been faulty. Thirty men and women in black formal dress stood awkwardly in a long gloomy room. Frozen in a moment of stillness, their mouths open as if their souls had just flown out of them, they were like expressionist figures in Nordic woodcuts.

As the pupils dilated to cope with the sudden darkness, they tended to light on Major McCambridge. He had with magician's deftness taken off his shoes, and was now standing on the dining-room table in his socks. An old copy of *Country Life* protected the mahogany table from possible soiling. He was fiddling with the wiring of the chandelier.

' Loose connection here, I think,' he shouted to the group who were staring up at him, like the Israelites waiting for the news from Mount Sinai.

Only Timmy Le Mercier remained outside the group round the table. He was refilling his glass while Colonel Strachan told him a story. He was both pouring and listening with careful interest.

' Would you like a screwdriver?' asked Hervey.

' No,' said McCambridge, but if you've got an ordinary screw terminal, the sort you get in an ironmongers' for a few pence – '

' I rather doubt it,' said Hervey.

' Oh well, I'll just tie the ends together then. Of course it really needs resoldering.'

McCambridge reached up on tiptoe. The lights came back on. The guests clapped. They looked as if they were performing some ancient dance circling round this tiptoeing tail-coated figure on its mahogany pedestal. Was McCambridge, bathed in the light of the chandelier, the Golden Calf being adored for his vulgar opulence by the empty-headed multitude? Or was he some dionysiac figure leading a circle of frenzied maenads? His energy, his obsesssion with decision were certainly intoxicating. As he jumped down from the table, he explained the fault in the wiring to Mrs Strachan. She blushed as he spoke to her.

And, thought George, if by a few commonplace words you could make a sensible middle-aged woman behave as if you had made a pass at her, you had achieved something. You had re-established the principle of action. You became the hero, and ceased to be the story-teller or the audience. And to be the hero, that was surely the thing.